GLITCHES & STITCHES:

DEATH VIOLATION 01

NICOLE GIVENS KURTZ

TABLE OF CONTENTS

COPYRIGHT

Glitches & Stitches: Death Violation 01

Electronic ISBN: 979-8-9873795-1-6

Print ISBN: 978-1-7371320-9-7

Short Story, "Sparks Out" Originally published in *Disharmony of the Sphere* in 2015.

Credits:

Cover art: Logan Keys
Editor: Rie Sheridan Rose
Proofreader: Misty Massey

CHAPTER ONE

THE DISTRICT'S rain-drenched streets and crumbling structures drowned between Monday's constant downpour and a gloomy Wednesday. Fawn Granger marched along the soaked sidewalks in her galoshes and yellow raincoat. As a kid she had liked splashing in the cold rain, feeling the spray against her bare legs. Now the memory of those happier times dissolved like sugar left out in a storm.

On the way to the scene, she'd reveled in the exhilaration as she puddle-jumped along The District's cracked and warped sidewalks. Overhead, the chilly afternoon squall held hints of a future snowfall once the temperature plummeted below freezing. October seesawed between frost and fall.

The sky could tell her everything except the identity of the rotting corpse waiting for her at the death violation. It was time to get down to business.

She approached the rubberneckers and media hogs

vying for gory content to consume. Social media remained insatiable, greedily devouring any- and everything and crapping on people's lives.

And their deaths.

The yellow caution beam sectioned off a quarter of a block including one lane of traffic. The beam prevented bystanders from getting close to the scene and swarming the area around the deceased and ruining evidence. Judging from the blaring horns and irate shouting, pilots didn't like it. Briscoe, her partner she affectionately called BB, yelled over to her as she dipped beneath it. "You swim here from your place?" Briscoe asked.

Why can't death be more convenient? Fawn shook her head. She pulled on the mask from her satchel. "What do we got?"

"One of the pedestrians said she heard shouting just after 1600 hours," Briscoe said.

Briscoe walked with her, slightly ahead, leading her to the deceased. He carried an umbrella in one hand, and a cigarette in the other. He'd come prepared for the weather in a dark gray coat, black turtleneck, and dark dress pants. He didn't fit with the flying wautos—wind automobiles—, robotic servers floating around the violation scene's parameter, and flutter of photographers. He looked like he'd stepped out of the Robert B. Parker online detective game's character list.

"You know, I already looked at the body. You don't have to—"

"I'm fine." She twisted her dreadlocks into a bun at the base of her neck. It kept her shoulder-length hair out of the way of the corpse. Nothing like getting blood, bile, and human baseness in your locks and the hell it took to get out. "But really, BB, smoking?" She took in a deep breath and squatted down beside the victim.

The person who used to be alive. He wore a round, laser-gun blast to the chest and expensive clothing too pricey to be from this section. It was a horrific sight. The violation scene techs buzzed around in their bright white one-piece suits with the VIO label on the back in black block lettering. Their equipment was waterproof, but the body was not.

"Can we get some protection over here? All our evidence is running off with the rain!" Fawn stood up.

"Yeah! Sorry!" A male, with an Afro of curls, shouted at one of the techs. "Marquise! Set up the canopy."

Her knees were soaked. *Great.* She stepped back to get her breath. The mask made breathing harder, but the burnt flesh from the laser-gun blast didn't help. She fought not to snatch the thing off her face and vomit. Contaminating a violation scene wouldn't look good on her evals, so she spun away from the corpse as a sour taste flooded her mouth. She closed her eyes to pause the world's tilt.

When she opened them again, two men hurried to set up the electronic devices on either side of the body. With a press of the buttons, a shimmering force field appeared like a dome. Rain ran over it and down the sides, away from the deceased.

She caught Briscoe frowning at her. His pursed lips forced the corners of his mouth downward.

"I told you I'd do it."

"And I said I'm fine."

"Liar."

"Those ashes can contaminate the scene. We've talked about this." Fawn gestured to his cigarette. Its round, red tip glowed in the gloomy late afternoon.

"I'm cutting back." He took a drag as if to prove his point.

"Who this is?" Fawn pointed at the body.

"Leonardo Cho, scientist with the Association of Genetically Engineered Humans." Briscoe took another long drag.

"What's he doing here? The AGEH's offices aren't even in this sector."

"And that's it. No partner. No kids. Extended family is out in the Tokyscio area. The Cali Province is always changing the names on those damn quadrants..." He caught himself and straightened out his coat. The ash fell into the rain puddles. "The Anderson Clinic's not too far from here. Maybe he worked there."

"Yeah, maybe. How'd he get here?" Fawn's rain-soaked pants had plastered themselves to her thighs. "A late-night street fight around here leaves one dead but from the looks of it, he still has all his organs. Too much spontaneous violence. Looks like he fought back too."

Briscoe shrugged. "Gonna have to wait for the vioTechs to get their work done."

"All right. Witnesses?"

"None human. vioTech's grabbing the video footage."

"This area is crawling with people. No one saw anything?"

"Most got their faces planted in their devices. You know?"

Fawn sighed. "Let's talk to the employer."

"The AGEH? See now, Fawn, I know the place looks progressive, but there is still some backwardness to how they do things," Briscoe explained. He twisted his lips as if the words tasted bad.

"I'm well aware of the things they do." Fawn heard the sharpness in her tone, but she wanted this resolved tonight. She knew exactly what the Association of Genetically Engineered Humans did. If the e-file journalists got hold of the story some tabloid snot like Malcolm Moore would ruin it. "And *backward* doesn't begin to cover it. Cruel. Deadly. Those adjectives would do."

"This is politically sensitive." Briscoe loosely crossed his arms where he could still hold the umbrella and smoke. "The District is in crisis, especially this sector. Add in the AGEH…"

"I'm not speaking of things you don't already know." Fawn met his eyes and watched him squirm beneath her gaze. "Our victim worked there."

"They're a not-for-profit medical *organization* whose primary focus is to enrich human beings through genetic manipulation. They conduct research to create and save lives." Briscoe countered.

"You write their damn website babble?" Fawn shook

her head. The smell of death made her stomach hurt, but thankfully the rain had washed away most of the odor.

"Life isn't about *finding* yourself, but about *creating* yourself. The AGEH creates people."

"I wonder what else they've created."

Briscoe leveled his gaze at her. "Not all of us can fly off into the Southwest. Many of us live here."

"Is that what you're put-out about?"

"You're splitting up our successful team. For a ranch."

She couldn't deal with this tonight. The District had drained her. Eight years had rendered her sparks out. The regulator AI had labeled her with PTSD and leaving the District would remove her from the trauma of regulator life. Her mother had been a regulator. She'd told Fawn when she first rookied for the District about the dangers of trying to shovel humanity's muck. It could cover you, and drown out one's spirit, their spark.

Burn. Explode. Ignite. Spark. But don't get snuffed out.

The bodies. She couldn't stop seeing them, even when asleep. So she'd stop doing a lot of sleeping.

"I'm not going to go through it again. This is our last one, so let's make it count," Fawn said, more to herself than Briscoe.

Without waiting for Briscoe's reply, she started for the supervising vioTech. They needed answers.

She also wanted to stop him from going on about the AGEH. They created hatchlings. In fact, Briscoe—being a hatchling—might be too close to the subject to be objective. The AGEH's image versus their reality clashed and when that happened, it jarred people—even genetically engineered ones.

Cameras clicked and scanners whirred as vioTechs worked their way around the body.

The tall, dark, and handsome vioTech stood just a way off from the body, writing on his tablet with a stylus —a bit of an old-fashioned techie. She liked that. Meant he got his hands dirty and didn't rely on the technology to give him all the answers.

"You're the new VIO lead?" Fawn asked once she reached him. She yanked her hood up as the rain fell harder. "I'm Inspector Regulator Fawn Granger."

Fawn held out her hand in greeting. He didn't extend his as he wrote with one, while his other gloved hand held the tablet. He wore the same raincoat as the others, but he carried himself with authority.

When he finished writing, he looked up at her.

"I'm Doctor Ryan Rycroft. The deceased, Mr. Cho, has been dead for 2 to 4 hours. Cause of death appears to be a laser-gun blast, but we still have toxicology reports to run. I'll need to open him up to know more. We found a trace of oil on his hands and a discarded umbrella. His fingermarks are on it. They're tacky so they didn't rinse off in the rain."

"Right down to business." Fawn pulled out her own tablet and took notes.

He watched her with intense eyes, and she didn't have to guess how he had become the VIOs supervisor. Quick, sharp intelligence shone in those eyes, along with a warning not to cross him.

"Thank you. You'll contact us when you get more." Fawn slipped her device back into her coat pocket.

"Of course," he replied. A small smile tugged at his lips.

"Thanks." Fawn headed back to the body, but seeing the vioTechs around it, decided she'd gotten enough. She ducked beneath the caution beam with Briscoe right behind her. They headed back down the sidewalk until the pulsating glow of the regulator wautos' lights vanished behind buildings.

"You think it's a hate violation?" Briscoe stopped at the crosswalk.

Overhead, wautos, aerocycles, drones, and cargo crafts all vied for air space. On the ground, the streets still went by their prewar names. In the air, folks went by coordinates. Still, accidents happened, so Fawn waited for the robotic controller to give them the white walking man before stepping off the curb and crossing the ground level street. Sometimes pilots lost control and landed in a ditch or a pile of people.

Once the light changed, they walked along with the throng, hurrying to escape the downpour. They rushed to the nearest shelter beneath the awning of a closed cafe.

Restaurants had gone the way of automobiles since the Great War that left the United States in shambles.

"You hear me?" Briscoe fumbled in his pocket and removed a vintage cigarette case. It matched his tele-monitor's case.

"I dunno." Fawn removed her hood. Everything was wet. Water ran down her back beneath her blouse. "We know Cho worked for the AGEH, but it might not be a factor in his death. We don't have enough of anything to jump to conclusions."

Briscoe nodded, his ebony hair perfectly in place. Tapered to the back, with long bangs in the front, his hair defied humidity. No facial hair, ever. Briscoe claimed it made him look ancient.

"How did he get down here?" Fawn searched around. "This isn't anywhere close to the AGEH office or his residence."

Briscoe pulled out his tablet. "According to the witness—a Jacob Munro, who works at the CC stop—Cho get off the craft at 1600 hours. VioTechs already pulled the cameras' video feeds and confirmed."

"So, he's alive at 1600 hours," Fawn repeated.

"The death violation was logged in at 17:12. Anonymous."

"He was killed shortly after leaving the cargo station stop." Fawn took in the area around. The cargo craft picked up and dropped off commuters. "It's wide open out here. No witnesses?"

"A mugging perhaps?" Briscoe suggested, but his expression told her he didn't believe it either. "No one saw anything, except Munro, and he didn't see the actual violation."

Mugging violations ranked among the lowest committed violations. No one carried real currency, not since before the war. So, attempting to steal items off of a person didn't make good profit for the violator. It took too long and was too messy to cut the chip out of someone's wrist. It happened, just not often.

Her hands shook, but she shoved them into her pockets, squeezed her eyes shut to close out the rising anxiety and fear. It crawled over her like a thousand ants. She shuddered despite her efforts to suppress it.

"You okay?" Briscoe touched her shoulder. "Fawn?"

"Let's get inside. I don't like talking in the open." Fawn adjusted her hood. Stormy and gathering dark, the evening lumbered on.

And a killer walked free.

CHAPTER TWO

TWENTY MINUTES LATER, Fawn and Briscoe reached The Cored Apple Restaurant. The server led them to a u-shaped, two-person booth. Savory scents hinted at the deliciousness served here. A mixture of human and robotic staff hummed in established routines in the sleek black and metallic décor. For being one of the few places to serve non-mutated beef, and supper time, the seating area remained almost empty.

"It smells great in here. You hungry?" Briscoe asked, folding his coat over the side of the booth. He moved the table's foghog toward him and took out a cigarette without looking.

"How can you eat after what we just saw?" Fawn folded her hands low, over her stomach. "I think a coffee will be it for me."

"How?" Briscoe lit the cigarette by placing it against the heat patch at the base of his case. Once it ignited, he held it between his fingers, and the round foghog sucked in the lavender-scented smoke.

"Yeah. How do you absorb it?"

"I put all of it aside and do my job. It's work." Briscoe scooted back in the seat and smoked.

"You dunno, do you?" Fawn said.

"Not at all. I just do it."

"Bonjour! Qu'allez-vous manger ce soir?" The server arrived at their table. He spoke in a hushed tone, and he held a tiny square device in his hand.

"Sythe Blackberry Tea." Briscoe crossed his legs. The creases of his pants were sharp enough to cut someone. His boots shined despite being wet from the rain. He leaned down and wiped away the damp with his handkerchief.

The server glanced at Fawn. *"Pour toi?"*

"Café, noir, avec poudre."

Once he left, Fawn crossed her arms and leaned on the table. They should be out working the case, but she needed a pause. The threat of a panic attack lingered, a cold shadow.

"Oh, crap on toast, I know that look." Briscoe rolled his eyes.

"What?"

"You have a hunch." Briscoe pointed an accusing finger at her.

"We got nothing."

"Bollocks," Briscoe whispered. "Dr. Rycroft's team is good. They found a beat-up umbrella next to the body. Well, a short distance away. It's got the victim's fingerprints on the handle. Based on the damage, he tried to fight off his attacker with it. It's bent all to hell."

"We don't know any more about him."

Briscoe arched an eyebrow. "No. Not yet. You know how these cases work. We're peeling the layers back to reveal the violators."

"We're at the first layer, still outside the fruit." Fawn scowled.

She'd conducted an initial social media sweep as she flew over to the restaurant, but she hadn't come up with anything except a few decades of images and blog posts.

Now drained, she wanted to go home and sleep, but she pushed through the gnawing fear. "It's impossible to exist without leaving some sort of electronic footprint. Currency. Medicine. Jet fuel. All of it comes and goes via wireless streams of information. How could information about him simply not be out there?"

Briscoe shrugged. "He's AGEH. Rumors are they scrub that stuff off the 'net."

"Damn Big Corporate Brother. It's a serious setback."

"I can call a contact."

"Who?" Fawn didn't like Briscoe's tone.

"Malcolm Moore, a freelancer for the *D.C. Mirror.* I've used him a few times in the past for information."

Fawn groaned. "Not him. The tabloid tipster. He's the worst."

"He has hundreds of snitches and contacts. The man's a physical internet."

Briscoe paused as the server dropped off their drinks. The slip of a man smiled politely at Fawn, but gave a full, bright flash of teeth to Briscoe. When he walked away, he gave Briscoe a tiny wave over his shoulder.

"BB, focus!" Fawn drummed her fingers on the table.

"Don't be jealous," Briscoe lifted his tea to his lips. He blew twice before sipping gingerly.

The coffee smelled great, but the lack of milk products available in the District meant she had to drink it black with powdered sugar. Not a complaint, but the limited amount of sugar blunted only some of its bitterness. It kept her from grimacing when she encountered life's bitter pills.

"We can get answers. We could use some of those." Briscoe pressed. Sometimes if he asked often enough Fawn relented.

"Yeah, but can we trust what he might give us?" Fawn sipped.

"We'll back it up with evidence." Briscoe nodded at her and sipped too.

Fawn put her cup down. "We keep what we can prove. Discard what we can't."

"Like always."

She signaled the waiter. "Like always."

An hour passed and brought with it pain. Fawn's agony pooled at the edges of her consciousness, but the complete picture remained out of focus. *Who shot Dr. Cho?* Only her throbbing headache remained despite the injection of pain reliever.

She rubbed her temples and tried to soothe the quiver

of restlessness inside her. She wanted to run, to dissolve on the spot, but that wouldn't find the violator.

After the impromptu meeting at The Cored Apple, Fawn returned to The District's Regulator Headquarters. It had consumed what was once the Federal Bureau of Investigations Building downtown. The District's territory boundaries had been extended beyond the original District of Columbia, absorbing parts of the former Virginia and Maryland states.

Fawn flew her regulator-issued wauto through the funnel. A mile-long force field protected the building and kept flying vehicles from plowing into it. Local traffic flew around it. Regulations ordered that the elevated lanes remain a certain distance from structures. A single-entry point forced all traffic through its central entranceways. Behind HQ, the rear had been converted to a parking lot for the fleet.

"Identification." The regulator's tone brooked no humor.

"Inspector Regulator Granger. ID Alfa36ZuluBravo." Fawn turned up the wind channel in the wauto to three. Her face felt hot.

"Voice print identified. Cleared."

Fawn flew around to the rear parking lot and set down in an open spot. As she made her way through security and up to the second floor, she pushed back against the urgency to crawl into a corner and curl herself into a ball. She entered her shared office and shrugged out of her coat. She hung it on the entranceway hooks, along with her satchel, and made a beeline to her desk.

Briscoe sat in his chair—a highback leather relic he'd won from Fawn's Nana in a bridge game. It looked at odds with the white desk, wall-size glass tele-monitor, and sleek embedded technology. His desk was situated closer to the door.

Fawn spied a man speaking to him on the tele-monitor.

Malcolm Moore appeared on screen with a broad grin and eager eyes. He sported a dark goatee and one shoulder-length plait. Behind him, a wall of monitors streamed footage from a variety of locations, in The District.

"Baker! Is Lomax with you?" Malcolm asked. "You got something for me?"

Fawn plopped down at her desk. She gripped the edges, but her sweaty fingertips caused her hands to slip off.

Briscoe shook his head. "I'm coming to you for info. You heard anything about Lucky Strange?"

"I don't know him. There haven't been any whispers, but I'll put out some feelers to see what the spyders catch in their webs," Malcolm said.

The oily journalist's nasal tone made the hairs on her neck stand up. The ache had taken up residence in the base of her neck and wrapped itself around her frontal lobe. Rubbing it did little to ease the pain. Normally, she'd go home when it got like this, but Fawn wanted the case resolved tonight.

Next week would be too late. She had to resolve Dr. Cho's violation. Laser-gun blasts to the chest weren't self-inflicted. The sooner she wrapped up the case, the sooner she could get away to the Southwest Territories.

So she forced herself to wait for Briscoe.

A year ago, Fawn worked a case in the Southwest and after some legal maneuverings managed to drag the suspect back to The District. Impressed by her skills, the Southwest Territory Regulators invited her out for a job. She accepted the offer. Each territory had their own way of governing. Laws, regulators, rules, and other manners to maintain order and battle back anarchy. The data they shared with her showed fewer death violations and more cyber ones. Less blood. More byte. Most of her items had been loaded onto a cargo craft and were on their way to her new ranch home outside of the Four Corners Quadrant. The noisy, violent heartbeat of The District would be far behind.

CHAPTER THREE

BRISCOE DISCONNECTED the visual with a flourish. He crossed his legs. In one hand, he held a cigarette and in the other his tablet. He peered at her across the neat expanse of his desk to the cluttered and crowded top of hers.

"You look like shit."

"Thank you, BB"

"Migraine?"

"My, aren't you the inspector." Fawn gave him a weak smile.

Stress. Too much violence. Too much blood. Too much vileness. When she blinked, she saw the bloody scene.

Briscoe laughed. "I'm assuming you have taken the injection?"

"Yeah. Give it time." Fawn winced. "Just tell me what you got."

He paused, released a sigh, and inhaled. "All right.

Moore said he will see what he can find."

"And?" Fawn closed her eyes.

"And, we have an appointment with the other AGEH research doctor, a Dr. Margie Baldwin, tomorrow."

"Great. I'm going home." Fawn pushed herself to a standing position. The wave of nausea threatened to cripple her.

"Good idea," Briscoe said. "I'm going to dig around a bit before knocking off for the night."

Without thinking, she hurried over to the exit, grabbed her satchel and raincoat with hardly a pause. It was like she walked on autopilot. Some other entity piloted her body. Inside her mind shouted, *Wait! We got a death violation to solve.*

"Fawn?" Briscoe said a blink before she headed out of their office.

"Let me know if anything turns up." Fawn flipped up the collar of her raincoat.

"Of course." Briscoe watched her with concern.

How could she explain the hollowness pressing against her heart or the void looming like a wide, waiting mouth ready to devour joy, hope, safety?

She made her way to the side door that led to the parking lot designated for personal vehicles. Both hands clutched her satchel, letting go only long enough to put on her helmet and launch the flight sequence. She climbed on her aerocycle, and launched into the elevated lanes. The autopilot clicked on, and she entered the coordinates for home.

She didn't trust herself to fly.

Sebastian, her black cat, greeted her at the door.

"Not now, Sebastian." Fawn dropped her satchel, coat, and shoulder holster in a heap just inside the doorway. Her fingers automatically reactivated the alarm. It deactivated when she entered her keycode and voice identification to open the door, but she liked it being on all the time. It had become habit—when the door hushed closed behind her, she turned the alarm back on.

Sebastian demanded his food, meowing loud and clear in their small kitchen.

"I know I'm late. Work. If I don't do it, *we* don't eat." Fawn walked over to the cabinet and took out a container of cat food. She opened it and set it out in front of Sebastian. "Here you go, boy."

As he ate, Fawn petted him. He liked having an audience. Vibrating like a small motor, Sebastian expressed his gratitude. Fawn's knees weakened, so she slid down to the floor.

After a few minutes, she removed her boots and headed to her bedroom. Once stripped of her damp clothing, she crawled into bed and burrowed under the covers. The dark, the warmth, and the security eased the thundering in her head.

"Finally, the medication's working." She sighed in relief.

Her mind wandered to the AGEH. They held disturbing beliefs, but they had the governor's backing and Congress's support. Their bizarre beliefs drove their directives, especially the research and development division. Their practices included alleged human experimentation, cybernetics, and ingestion of non-regulated nanobots. The AGEH was an inconceivable evil, but they made a lot of currency. It eased people's outrage.

Fawn's body relaxed into the lush sheets and her pillow's soft comfort. As an inspector, she spent too much of herself battling bad people; once she arrived home, she wanted to be enveloped in a cocoon. The next morning she'd emerge renewed.

That was *if* she could get to sleep.

She peeked out from under the covers and peered at the sleep aid vial on her nightstand. It would help her fall asleep, sure, but the issue didn't fade when she slept. It was full of pitfalls and challenges. The lingering, achy pain didn't go away. The nightmare put its tentacles into her body, transporting her back to the scenes of butchered corpses and violent encounters. She woke with a racing heart and sweat-soaked sheets.

Tonight, she closed her eyes and tried to get some natural sleep.

Yet a sense of urgency pressed upon her like a cold ice pack against her back.

"Andre, play summer rain." Fawn burrowed back under the covers.

Her home AI valet launched the program—a white noise of rain drumming on a wooden surface.

Fawn sighed. *Why? Why was Dr. Cho at the cargo stop? If he was on his way to a clinic, why was he going in at 4 in the afternoon?*

Fawn rolled over, but the whirling thoughts and questions followed.

She peered out of her blanket fort again to the nightstand. The clear liquid beckoned with its promise of relief and rest. Maybe, if she took a large enough dose, she could get peace. An extended slumber so she could put her burdens down for good.

Meow. Sebastian leapt onto the sea of blankets.

"Really!" Fawn bolted upright. "Give a warning next time."

The black cat blinked his green eyes in apology before making his way up the bed's length to Fawn. Without warning, he rubbed his face against Fawn's naked chest, purring as he did so. His whiskers tickled her. She giggled and scooped him up, cradling him like an infant.

"You rotten boy." She rained kisses onto his head.

Sebastian soaked it in and purred his delight.

"Thank you."

He wiggled out of her embrace. He'd had enough.

"Well, fine. Your breath smells like tuna," Fawn teased.

Sebastian meowed and kneaded the covers close to Fawn.

"Watch your language, sir," she laughed.

As she scooted back under the covers, she glanced at the bottle of sleeping aid. The drumming of rain harmonized well with Sebastian's bass level purring. The anxiety rolled back as if in fear of being drowned out.

Fawn laid down to sleep.

Briscoe watched Fawn until she disappeared into the stairwell. His handheld beeped. Once he fished it out of his pocket, Raul's smooth, angular face appeared.

"Hey, honey," Briscoe said.

"*Hola*! I got a small break. I wanted to see how you were holding up. Heard from some medics about a death violation over by F Street." Raul ran a hand through his curly brown hair. His wrinkled scrubs meant he'd been busy with surgeries. A mask adorned his neck.

"We're working it."

"We? I thought Fawn withdrew from service."

"Her last day is Friday."

"You don't sound excited."

Briscoe shrugged. Of course, he wasn't thrilled. Their partnership had become close over the last five years.

"BB, considering her, uh, challenges, this kind of work can't be good for her mental health."

The last few years had kept Briscoe walking on eggshells, but he didn't mind it.

"Fawn's mental health matters more than anything. If she falters, we can't resolve the death violation. Worse still, the captain may reassign her and give me another partner."

To hell with that.

"Apparently, she has other plans anyway. Jetting off to the Southwest, leaving The District, leaving me," Briscoe said.

Raul smirked. "If this move helps her become healthier, why are you angry, babe? Be happy. You just said it matters more than anything."

"I know, but I'll miss her."

"You still got me." Raul blew him a kiss.

"Forever. Now, how're things at the hospital?" Briscoe swallowed the knot of emotion, glad to shift the conversation to something else.

He wiped his brow.

On screen, Raul became somber. "Busy. Three wauto wrecks, a few overdoses, and a fatal self-inflicted laser-gun wound…to a child…"

Briscoe cringed. All that carnage and all before noon—and those were just those Raul worked on, not the others arriving in the emergency room.

"How are *you* holding up?

"That's my line! I'm better now." Raul managed a tiny grin. "You gonna make it home on time tonight? I'm thinking wheat pasta with bell peppers and tofu in a savory marinara sauce. I know we got a decent red in the cellar."

"I'll be home on time if you only make lettuce," Briscoe said.

Surgery wasn't the only thing Raul excelled at with his hands. He moonlighted on weekends as a chef. When he became stressed, he cooked, which—due to the nature of his job—was nearly every night.

"See you later. Be safe."

"You too. Love you."

"Ditto." Raul winked and disconnected.

Alone in the office, Briscoe reviewed what they had on Dr. Leonard Cho. Victimology could help them narrow down or at least unearth suspected violators. He double tapped on the screen and an image of Cho appeared. Using a stylus, he wrote the following:

Doctor Leonard Cho

Born: January 7, 2100Age: 49Citizen: Yes

Origin: Cali ProvenceSiblings: NoneParents: Deceased Employer: AGEH

Briscoe sighed. They hadn't discovered a sibling in the files from the Tokyosci Police. Uniform Regulators had spoken to the extended family: two aunts, a cousin, and three uncles. They hadn't spoken to Cho in months, which according to them was normal. *Who was in Cho's circle?*

"Baker," came from behind him.

Briscoe turned to find Inspector Regulator Colin Neese stood beside Fawn's desk. He had one hand in his pocket. His black laser-gun holster blended into his dark sweater.

"Where's Granger? Gone already to the wide, open spaces? This must be a hard loss for you." Neese jutted his chin at Fawn's empty chair.

"Chasing down a lead." Briscoe closed the gap between them. "What do you want?"

Neese didn't give bytes about him or Fawn.

Neese's facial tattoos flickered. Briscoe wondered what information they contained—a daughter's first word, a favorite song, or a deceased loved one's voice.

"Don't be like that. We're all on the same side." Neese flashed a toothy grin.

"Except when you're shirking duties to go snitch on Fawn—one of us." Briscoe crossed his arms to keep from punching the nerve out of his colleague. "Your words don't carry weight."

"She was a *danger* to the whole team! It's not my fault she surged and started firing on every-damn-body. She nearly hit Daniel!" Neese leaned into Briscoe's personal space. "I won't apologize for saving lives. I don't know why the admins let her come back, but know this—if she surges again, I will *delete* her."

"Get your affairs in order, then, because you'll follow behind her." Briscoe held Neese's gaze. Fire burned in his belly and spread through him as it roared back to him.

Neese's terrible, shoddy investigation had landed them in a gun battle with better armed violators. Fawn's mental health failed amidst the shouting, the blood, and the bodies. She dissolved into a brief period of hallucinations and terror.

The air intensified and the atmosphere circled them. Rumors said Neese's sneaky nature meant he'd sell his mom for promotion and favor. Their clashes over the past five years demonstrated nothing else.

After a few moments, Neese gave him another toothy grin.

"A somewhat cryptic message, Baker. Since you won't say what you mean, I'm gonna answer your question," Neese said, his lips peeled back in a sneer. "I came by to give you some background on Leonard Cho. From the looks of your board, you can use it."

Briscoe didn't smile. Instead he returned to his desk.

Neese followed. "Look, do you want the info or not?"

"Where's it from?"

"Me."

Briscoe gestured for him to go ahead. He pressed the record button on his desk.

With a glance at the glowing button, Neese hesitated.

"Go on, IR Neese. Share your tip. I appreciate you working collaboratively with us."

Neese scowled at the mocking tone. "Cho worked primarily at the Anderson Clinic. About six months ago, we grabbed a hacker during a routine investigation into a death violation. She'd gotten into their R & D database and managed to snatch some pretty damning intel, a real treasure trove..."

"...While committing a series of violations." Briscoe stood. He wiped his palms on his slacks. *How trustworthy can this intel be?*

Neese put his hands on his hips and his eyes darted to the door, then back to Briscoe. "Info on the victim, Dr. Cho, and his project. She found some interesting things about him."

"What's her name?" Now Briscoe's attention had been snared. He felt sick to his stomach. Anything to do with the AGEH was suspect.

"Damoni Brees from Sector 12."

"What cradle are they sleeping in?"

Neese leaned back against Fawn's desk. "She's not. Although she had inconsistencies in her statement, the attorney couldn't make the violations stick. Currency was put into her account and all violations were dissolved."

Briscoe stopped the recording. His suspicions changed.

"You independently corroborated her data?"

"Yeah."

"Where's the confiscated data?"

"Gone. Lost." Neese smirked.

"Lost," Briscoe repeated, using his fingers to form air quotes around the word.

"Damoni might have copies. You know hackers. They hoard."

CHAPTER FOUR

TUESDAY MORNING, Fawn stood beside her assigned regulator wauto.

"You're flying." She adjusted her weapon harness on her shoulder to stop it from digging into her muscle.

"Too early for you?" Briscoe wore dark glasses, a black turtleneck, and his elegant navy trenchcoat. It had silver geometric shapes against its dark background. "If I'm flying, then we're using my wauto."

"Fine."

They marched across the rows of vehicles over to the employee's personal vehicle lot. Briscoe slid into the pilot's soft leather seat. Fawn eased into the passenger one. "I love this wauto," she commented.

Briscoe's automated seatbelt clicked into place. "Me too."

Fawn rubbed her gloved hands together. "It's freezing."

"You should've worn more than that little pea-coat and a tee-shirt."

Fawn ignored him and flipped the heat on. Chilly air streamed out to greet her.

"You have to wait on warmth." Briscoe laughed, as he flew them the short distance to the Anderson Clinic.

"You're in a jovial mood." Fawn took her tablet from her coat's inner pocket.

"I shared the audio from my talk with Neese. He came to the office after you left."

Fawn grimaced. Her stomach became queasy. "What'd he want?"

"He gave me a tip to follow up on. A hacker supposedly got some R & D information from the AGEH, and said intel included Cho's projects."

Fawn quirked an eyebrow. "Oh? Did he have alcohol on his breath when he told you?"

"No, but it was savage. How does such a handsome man have such atrocious halitosis?"

Fawn playfully slapped his arm. "BB!"

Briscoe summarized what Neese had said.

Once he finished, Fawn said, "We should talk to her."

"For sure. I searched. There weren't a lot of people in Cho's life. He appears to be a loner. The extended family haven't heard from him in about six months, and it was spotty."

"How was he the last time they talked to him?"

Briscoe signaled a change of lanes to make the left. "They said he acted normal—well, for him. He was excited about a new breakthrough he'd made, but when one of the aunties pressed him about the details, he clammed up, citing AGEH regulations."

"Humph. Who benefited from his death?" Fawn glanced up and surveyed the passing landscape.

"No one we've found so far except a cousin." Briscoe blew a few smoke rings. "She gets his possessions. Cho didn't have any money in his currency accounts. His victimology is pretty thin."

"So he was married to the job."

"Yeah."

"There's got to be something, *someone*. What's his role at the Anderson Clinic?" Fawn scrolled through the data folder housing the case file. She scanned the notes Briscoe had uploaded to the file. "It's not here."

"I couldn't get anything out of them except he worked there." Briscoe set the autopilot and stuck another cigarette in his mouth. He activated the foghog before lighting it.

"They're going to be difficult. Businesses usually treat employees as property."

Fawn's belly dropped as the autopilot drifted lower to the ground as they approached the designated coordinates.

"Captain said don't piss off any important people," Briscoe said.

Fawn *tsked*. "It's like he doesn't know me."

Minutes later, they landed in an available parking spot a few spaces from Anderson Clinic. They exited the vehicle. Fawn hunched further into her coat and braced against the cold, fall breeze. Ahead of them, the clinic groaned beneath the weight of its history. The flickering neon sign of the former pizza place next door seemed on the edge of fading but blinked as if sending a frantic coded message before falling dark for good.

Briscoe said, "Damn, I should've brought the reg wauto. Mine may be stripped down to its wind turbine before we get out of the interviews."

"This is the place where they found out the AGEH had been performing experimental research on those teenage girls?" Fawn's vision blurred around the edges.

Briscoe exhaled smoke rings. "Allegedly. I bet Damoni Brees has the goods on them."

"She's gone to ground if you're right." Fawn pursed her lips. "Let's go."

"After you." Briscoe dropped his cigarette and ground it out with his high currency shoes.

Fawn and Briscoe walked up the flat cement stairs to the clinic doors.

The automatic doors yawned open, as the odor bowled her over. It didn't smell like anything clean occurred in this so-called place of healing. The people in the lobby didn't stir as they entered. Fawn's heart pinched at the despair and outright desperation weighing on them. Several wore the blank expressions associated with trauma victims, all in the name of science research. The AGEH had the reputation for using people as guinea pigs. Primarily from people hurt by their experiments.

Allegedly.

Briscoe marched up to the receptionist's desk. A woman the size of Mount Everest barked out answers to his quiet questions.

Her decibel level made Fawn's headache throb. She wouldn't skip coffee again. Wincing, she turned her attention to the people in the lobby. Ages ranged from infant to elderly, but all had hints of color in their skin, from tan to deep mahogany. Worn clothing, weathered faces, and withered hopes awaited the healing doctors behind the spotless, frosted-glass examination doors. Those ivory lab coats could take all the pain and the disease away.

Fawn folded her arms across her chest. Hope made a fickle mistress.

"Boo!" Briscoe whispered into her ear.

"BB!" Her hand went to her baton.

"Sorry. I forgot about the headache."

"*You* are a headache!" Her hand relaxed.

Briscoe raised his eyebrows. "We're going to interview the doctor, not beat her into submission."

Fawn shrugged. "The AGEH aren't known for being forthcoming."

Briscoe laughed. "Touché."

He took out a new cigarette but caught the furious scowl on the receptionist's face and put it back into its case. Fawn muffled a giggle, and winced at the sharp stab of pain in her temple. Damn.

The receptionist bellowed from her seated position at her desk. "Inspector Regulators Baker and Granger. Dr. Baldwin will see you now."

Mumbles rose at her declaration.

Briscoe and Fawn headed for the examination doors.

"Guess we aren't very popular here." Briscoe looked at Fawn.

"Guess not. People don't like regs. So you should be used to it."

When the doors opened, a waif of a woman—all bones and beauty—dressed in a white lab coat, creamy slacks, and hunter green sweater headed toward them. Her heels clicked on the tile floor. Long, brunette hair secured into a ponytail bounced as she walked. She held a tablet in one hand, and her other hand was extended for a handshake.

"Greetings, regulators. Terrible news about Dr. Cho. I'm Dr. Baldwin."

Fawn shook, as did Briscoe. She had a firm handshake.

"It's alarming," Fawn agreed. "I'm Inspector Regulator Granger. This is IR Baker."

"Follow me."

Dr. Baldwin walked down the corridor. Fawn and Briscoe followed. On this side of the doors, the odor of cleaning agents scrubbed the horrible dirty smell from the air. The lingering hint of loss remained. Bright, shiny, and hygienic masked the underlying smell of fear that permeated from behind closed examination room doors.

"We want to see Dr. Cho's workspace." Fawn removed her device from her pocket

"Of course." Dr. Baldwin smiled, but a slight hesitation caused lines to appear on her face. The tiny tug of her lips gave it all away.

They made a right and approached a glass-enclosed

workspace with eight-foot walls. Dr. Baldwin activated the retinal scanner, and the doors opened on a maze of square, glass cubicles. Biohazard signs dotted the cubicle doors. Large, rectangular tables—a few metallic, others smart-glass—dotted the room, stools encircling them. The first sectioned table space held microscopes, tubs, petri dishes, and gloves. Behind the tables, robotic parts occupied shelves. Around the hushed area, robots labored on what appeared to be n-bots, nursing robots.

Everyone had a robot. Robots were servitude and manual labor. They performed both the menial and massive tasks. N-bots, or nurse robots, handled medical assistance for minor things from colds and flu to setting broken bones and non-life-threatening wounds. Despite their mass production and inclusion in everyday life, the e-news files held at least one story daily about robots malfunctioning and causing serious injury.

The employees came in all shapes, sizes, shades, and status levels, though Fawn doubted anyone below citizen level had clearance to work for the AGEH. All spoke in quiet, conversational tones. She noted no one gave them any eye contact, strange, or questioning looks, as if regulator visits happened every day.

Perhaps they did.

A more logical reason was the employees had been briefed to shut up and look busy.

Or else.

"Did you work with Dr. Cho?" Briscoe brought Fawn back to their trio.

"Yes, Dr. Cho worked with several teams here," Dr. Baldwin answered over her shoulder.

"What did he do here? What's his official title and position?" Briscoe increased his walking speed to catch up with the doctor.

Dr. Baldwin made a right into the next aisle. "Dr. Cho was director of robotic development, his specialty being nurse bots."

"Did he work with anyone frequently? A team?" Fawn asked.

"Here you are." Dr. Baldwin turned and gestured to the glass table.

Briscoe smirked. "Can you tell me what Dr. Cho was working on?"

Her big green eyes widened behind her rimless glasses. "It's highly complex, Mr. Baker."

"*Inspector Regulator* Baker. Please, indulge me." Briscoe smiled, but it held little warmth. "We came here expecting transparency."

"You do know the regulations surrounding AGEH restricted access to research and development? I cannot reveal details of Dr. Cho's research. They are kept in a tightly-controlled environment. It has already been turned over to other scientists." Dr. Baldwin crossed her arms.

"Who are the new scientists?" Fawn stepped in closer.

"Olivia Hart...and myself. She's in the Midwest Territories."

"Where were you between the hours of 16:00 and 19:00?" Briscoe interjected.

She shot Briscoe another plastered-on smile. "I was

here. My coworkers can confirm. Security can confirm when I disconnected from the network."

"Tell us about Dr. Cho," Fawn chimed in. She had expected the AGEH to protect its secrets, but she wanted to know more about the victim. Briscoe seemed determined to push people until he got results. But one got farther with honey than with vinegar.

Dr. Baldwin huffed. "Right. Dr. Cho was the foremost authority on robotics. He would spend hours tracing his ideas on the ceilings' molding as if he could find all the secrets of the universe on them. We are all made of stars, but for Dr. Cho, life began in circuits."

"Cybernetics is a District violation." Fawn scribbled in her tablet.

"Indeed. I was only providing background for Dr. Cho." Her hands tightened on her tablet. "His work specifically applied to the n-bots while he was here."

"What about friends? Partners?" Briscoe looked inside Dr. Cho's workspace.

"We don't discuss those things." Dr. Baldwin's posture changed. Her coloring paled. A coldness crept into her eyes.

She's lying. Fawn looked at Briscoe out the corner of her eye, and back at the doctor.

"After work, then?"

Dr. Baldwin's smile waned a little. "No, but he struggled socially. Many here keep themselves to themselves and their projects. We promote teamwork and collaboration. Some employees are more successful than others, of course."

"I would like to talk to the team members from his recent project."

Dr. Baldwin stiffened, her face tight.

"We can get clearance, doctor. This is a death violation," Fawn pressed.

Dr. Baldwin released a deep sigh. Her hold on her patience lessened. Fawn had seen similar expressions on Captain Brinnington's face when dealing with her and Briscoe.

The clanging of metal caught Dr. Baldwin's attention. She twirled around. "Inspector Regulator Baker!"

Briscoe froze. He held two of what looked like robotic arms in his hands. "These are interesting."

Dr. Baldwin took them from him and replaced them on the shelves. "Please do not disturb this area."

"Oily," Briscoe remarked, then took out a handkerchief and rubbed his hands. His eyes flickered to Fawn. He mouthed the word *clue*.

Fawn gave a slight nod. "Come on, Sherlock." Then to Dr. Baldwin, "Our apologies."

Dr. Baldwin stood up from positioning the items back on the shelves. "What else can I help you with?"

"You could start by actually being helpful. I can come back with a judge's clearance and go through this entire facility, and what we find, we publish. With this clinic's reputation, it won't be a push to get a judge to grant it. I want the name of those coworkers."

Dr. Baldwin's smile dissolved into a thin slash of scarlet. "I do not haggle."

"Oh, I'm not haggling. Your colleague is dead. We'll get answers. Your help would be appreciated."

Dr. Baldwin hugged her tablet against her chest. "Our attorneys will be notified."

"A man is *dead*!" Briscoe threw up his hands.

Dr. Baldwin started, but regained her composure. "His death has nothing to do with this facility."

"He took a laser-gun blast to the chest." Fawn watched for some reaction, but Dr. Baldwin maintained her professional mask. "You can't be sure it doesn't connect to his work here."

"Are the AGEH that indifferent to their employees?" Briscoe leaned back against the table.

"Of course not," Dr. Baldwin scoffed.

"The AGEH has been accused of far worse. I recall Governor Price's mad scientist plot to create an army of super-engineered humans." Fawn picked up one of the p-drives on the table, and Dr. Baldwin took it from her hand.

"Ancient history and exaggerated rumor, Inspector Regulator Granger."

Briscoe pushed off from the table. "Look, you're giving out a whole lot of rumor right now, too."

Dr. Baldwin flinched at Briscoe's tone. She blinked as if seeing him for the first time. "Are you a hatchling?"

Briscoe touched his turtleneck. "How can you tell?"

Dr. Baldwin's mask slipped just a bit. "I create hatchlings. I can always tell. I don't need to see the mark."

"Dr. Cho." Fawn tapped on the glass table to keep them on topic.

"Yes, of course. Dr. Cho did not have a wife, children, or partner that I'm aware of. His personnel files do not list any either."

"Enemies?" Briscoe asked.

Dr. Baldwin shook her head. With an icy calm, she said, "None. As I said before, we foster an environment of collaboration, mutual respect, and teamwork. Without those we cannot create new robotics, genetic medicines, and advancements to aid mankind."

"You used so many buzz words, I'm spinning," Fawn said.

"You said a lot, and nothing, Dr. Baldwin. I'm impressed," added Briscoe.

"If there's nothing further, security can see you out." Dr. Baldwin hitched her chin up.

"Wait. Who are Cho's teammates?" Fawn forced a light casualness to her tone, the opposite of Briscoe's annoyed glare.

"It's a simple question. Why the reluctance with answering it?" Briscoe asked.

"You said you value teamwork. Dr. Cho couldn't be a team of one…" Fawn added.

A ping notification from Dr. Baldwin's tablet interrupted them.

"Excuse me." Dr. Baldwin read something on her tablet's screen. Her knuckles turned white, stark against the dark device's surface. Her lips pursed as if she'd eaten something sour.

"Friends?" Fawn asked.

"That's all the information I can provide. Please contact our attorneys with any additional questions. Security will see you out."

As she walked away, a pair of robotic guards

approached. They drifted with sharp precision to Fawn and Briscoe.

"This way please," they said in unison.

Their non-human voices raised goosebumps across Fawn's arms. Their ebony-painted bodies held bright yellow caution stars around their wide bases. Two arms gestured the direction Fawn and Briscoe should walk. The difference between man and machines had become blurry —neither had any original or independent thoughts.

"Thank you for your time," Fawn shouted to Dr. Baldwin.

"I think we can find our way back," Briscoe said to the bots.

"This way, please."

They followed security out a side door and into the light drizzle. The two egg-shaped guards waited until the door shut and locked before disappearing back into the clinic.

Fawn and Briscoe walked down the alley and around to the front of the clinic. The rain started to pick up, determined to douse The District. They raced toward the wauto and got in just before the sky opened in earnest.

Briscoe lit a cigarette. "Dead end."

"I don't think so. We know Dr. Cho was hiding something, and we know he had a team we need to talk to." Fawn shoved her hands into her coat's pockets. "The killing was clearly personal."

Briscoe quirked an eyebrow above the smoke. "Professional envy?"

"We need more on Dr. Cho."

"Hold up." Briscoe dug into his jacket and fished out his telemonitor. "Call coming in."

The sky opened more. The thundering rain drummed on the vehicle, and Briscoe covered with his hand. His telemonitor sat cradled in his lap.

VioTech supervisor Dr. Rycroft peered out from the screen. She couldn't hear what he was saying over the hammering torrent. Briscoe resorted to using an earpiece.

When he terminated the call, Briscoe blew out a hard sigh. "Rycroft said they have a few things we should see back at the station."

"Humph, she contacted you." Fawn crossed her arms. "BB, I think I need your cologne."

Briscoe laughed. "I'm sure she plugs into a different port."

"Or has both capabilities," Fawn countered. "Anyway, I wanna come back here. I wanted Dr. Baldwin to tell the me the truth, but since that was a bust, I want to see if I can catch one of the employees outside of work."

Briscoe wiped droplets from his face as they lifted up into the elevated lanes with a loud *whoosh.*

"I dunno. The CCTV catches you, or them talking to you, it can cause trouble for them. We got to go by HQ to get your areocycle anyway. Might as well see Rycroft."

Fawn shuddered from a chill. Goosebumps blanketed her arms. Damp and cold created a numbing feeling. October rain poured liquid misery on the territory. None of which helped her new budding headache. She reclined the seat, turned up the heat, and closed her eyes.

"I got a few pain patches in the medbox," Briscoe said.

"Use the damn foghog, BB."

He took her hand. Moments later, a cool, sticky pain patch covered the back of her left hand.

"Go little nanos," Briscoe cheered. "Make Fawn feel better."

"Thank you."

"I dunno how you can break us up. We're basically married."

Fawn heard Briscoe's hurt running along the edge of his forced amused tone. "Raul would have something to say about that."

Despite his faux cheeriness, Briscoe had been wounded by her decision, deeper than she'd realized. She hadn't seen it coming, because, well, she assumed he'd be happy for her.

He wasn't.

"Someone *there* knows more. Leonard Cho practically lived there. You saw his work space. No family images or hobbies. Nothing of interest beyond robotics. This was personal. His life was AGEH, so the answer's with them."

CHAPTER FIVE

SOMETHING about the smell inside Dr. Ryan Rycroft's vioTech lab reminded Fawn of the Anderson Clinic. The odor of death reeked in the autopsy room. He greeted them at the doorway and handed them masks.

"Thank you for getting down here so quickly." Dr. Rycroft called up Dr. Cho's internal scans on his smart-glass. It occupied the wall behind the body.

"We were in the sector," Fawn said from just inside the entrance to the first autopsy bay.

Dr. Rycroft held his tablet in one gloved hand and gestured toward the body with the other. Briscoe stood by the body, but Fawn remained at the end of the row of stainless-steel tables which lined the room. Others worked on bodies in hushed tones with quiet focus. They spoke into microphones and tiny cameras recorded their movements.

Dr. Cho's body. A dark cloth covered all of him except his head on the autopsy table. He looked at peace.

Like everything else in life, looks were deceiving.

"We have confirmed this is Leonard Hosek Cho." Rycroft pulled a hanging light closer to the body. "No one came to visually identify him. It's heartbreaking."

"Every death is to someone, doctor," Fawn said.

Rycroft gave her a small nod. "I guess, but to have no one—and only 50 years old..."

"He has family in Cali," Briscoe said.

Rycroft's soft features changed as he checked his notes. "Once we retrieved the body, and got him back here, I could see these abrasions on his face better. At first, I thought they were debris from when he collapsed to the ground, but on closer inspection, you can see these markings are embedded in his skin, especially here on his right cheek. Someone smashed his face with something that has this pattern."

"What made the marks?" Briscoe crouched down for a closer view. Fawn held her mask and her position.

"I'm not sure. We're working on identifying it," Rycroft said. "Someone with overwhelming rage killed him. Initially, I thought him an unlucky victim of a mugging, but quick grab violators don't spend this kind of time. They slice off your hand and keep going. This looks more sinister."

"What makes you say that?"

"Well, in addition to the facial injury, he has the laser-gun blast in his lower torso you saw at the crime scene." Dr. Rycroft turned to the scans and pointed to the torso. "That is the fatal injury. We're still attempting to identify the type of gun. The interesting thing here is that it's not from any laser-gun in our current inventory."

Fawn stepped closer to see the scans.

Briscoe looked up from his tablet. "Could it be from another territory?"

"Sure. As you know, inspector, not all territories keep records of gun owners, the sale of weapons, or if they were used in prior violations."

"So, you're saying it's a needle in a haystack." Fawn crossed her arms.

"Correct, IR Granger, but not impossible. It'll take time, so I wouldn't rely on this piece of evidence." Rycroft almost smiled, but it faltered when Fawn didn't return it. "But there's more."

He walked to the other side where a different scan appeared. He swept his finger across the JPEG, enlarging it. "The oil in the wound is a synthetic blend used in n-bots."

Briscoe pulled out his handkerchief. "Ah! Oil. Can you get this substance analyzed?"

"Sure." Dr. Rycroft left and then returned with an evidence bag. He accepted the stained cloth, sealed the bag, and wrote intake information with a permanent marker he kept in his lab coat pocket. "Where did you get this?"

Briscoe told him.

"We'll get it analyzed."

"Good," Fawn said.

"Our victim fought for his life. His blood was found on the umbrella, and he's got defensive wounds and lacerations on his forearms and hands."

"Could it be anything else?" Fawn peered through slits at the scan.

"Definitely violation," Dr. Rycroft said, turning to face them. "Method of death—exsanguination."

"Anything else?" Fawn started for the door.

"Yes. IR Granger, you don't look well."

"I'm fine."

"You're wearing a pain patch."

"Yeah…it helps."

"If you want, I can give you a quick check up…"

"Can you get me a cup of coffee?" Fawn asked, closing her eyes once more. *You've been touching dead bodies all day. Ew.*

"Yes, I can."

"Really?" Briscoe said.

Fawn's eyes flapped open. She couldn't physically contain her surprise.

"You didn't expect him to say yes, did you?" Briscoe laughed at her.

Dr. Rycroft removed his protective glasses, his gloves, and turned off the scans before he walked over to his inner office. It sat at the front of the autopsy bay, but it had a door and shades in case he wanted privacy from the business of autopsy.

Fawn didn't follow the doctor into his office. Instead, she and Briscoe spilled out into the hallway outside the bay. He guided her to a bench.

"Sit here. Did you sleep at all last night?"

"I did, but it was choppy as hell," Fawn said and crossed her arms over her chest.

"You haven't eaten. It's afternoon."

"BB, it's a caffeine headache," Fawn said. "I'm fine."'

"Okay. Okay." He raised both hands in mock surrender.

"Oh! There you are," Dr. Rycroft came toward her with a green mug of steaming coffee.

The rich aroma reached her before she registered him.

"*Merci*." Fawn took the mug from him.

"Careful, it's hot, and I put in an espresso shot to give you a boost. Drink it all. Doctor's orders."

"All your patients are dead," Briscoe said.

"I still know how to keep people alive, IR Baker," Dr. Rycroft answered. "I will contact you when I have more. We're processing evidence 24/7. It's busy."

"*Merci*," Briscoe said. "*Ciao*."

Fawn savored the dark java. It tasted good and hot against her throat. She felt the espresso almost instantly. "Oh, yes."

"Better?" Briscoe raised an eyebrow in question.

"Much."

"Excellent." Dr. Rycroft returned to the autopsy bay.

Relishing the bold flavor, Fawn drank more, wincing at its temperature. She stood up.

"Let's go check out Cho's residence," she said. "Then grab lunch."

"What are we looking for? I mean, vioTech's cleared it." Briscoe followed her to the elevator. Fingermark smears marred the surface.

"We need to find other means to locate people who knew him. I can't believe no one knew this guy. There may be clues in his apartment." Fawn's headache had started to recede. Now it didn't hurt so much to *think*.

They rode up to the first floor, stepped out, and ran into Neese.

"Granger! Good to see you walking around this place." He shot her a wide, but cold grin. "Baker."

Fawn uttered an "excuse me" and pushed by him.

"Hold up." Neese followed them, letting the elevator door close.

"What do you want?" Briscoe spun around, placing himself between Neese and Fawn.

Neese tried to peer over Briscoe's shoulder to see Fawn more clearly. "I—I wanted to see how you were getting on with finding Damoni."

"We've been chasing down evidence," Briscoe said, keeping his girth between Neese and Fawn.

At the sharpness in Briscoe's tone, Neese cocked his head at him. "It's a legitimate lead. She's worth talking to. That's a very nice coat, Baker. Bella Ado. Last season. Right?"

Briscoe ignored the dig. He loved his plush, ornate coat. "How would you know where Damoni is? You said you couldn't find her."

"Right. See, I have a few snitches in Sector 11, and they've spotted her around a place called *Bantu's*. We pulled the visuals from there, and *oui*, it's her."

"Why?" Fawn came around Briscoe.

Flustered, Neese fell back a step. "I guess 'cause she likes the food? The coffee? I dunno."

"No, why are you telling *us*? What do you get out of it?"

Briscoe smirked. "I asked him the same thing and he said 'we're all on the same side.'"

Neese snatched down the bottom of his blue sweater. "That's it. I'm being collaborative by sharing information. There's a death violator out there."

"I'm sure you don't know the meaning of the word, collaborative." Fawn walked off before Neese could say another word.

Briscoe growled at Neese before following Fawn down the hallway.

Once out in the parking lot, Fawn swore. "Screw him!"

Briscoe let her vent, as they climbed in his wauto.

When she'd finished, he said, "At least the rain slacked up a bit."

"Yeah. We *should* try to talk to Damoni Brees. If she's got intel on Cho and the AGEH, we may need it. It wouldn't hurt to expand our questioning."

"I don't trust Neese."

"Me neither."

"You know, it isn't all that surprising Cho doesn't have any real-world friends. Think about it, Fawn. Who do you associate with—in person? Me, a work colleague. Your family is in the Southwest too, right?"

Fawn nodded.

"We all kind of enter our mouse holes and blither around before emerging for another day. We work with people, but the bulk of The District's workforce is remote. People don't have to leave their homes—for anything. Food is ordered online, friends are online, doctor's online, entertainment's online, hell *life* is online."

"True, but Cho worked in an office, with people. He lived in his apartment with neighbors..."

Briscoe said, "You're saying someone saw something. If they didn't the building's surveillance probably did."

Fawn said, "And that someone may have killed him."

CHAPTER SIX

DR. CHO'S loft sat on the fifth floor of a warehouse turned into apartments during the last century. Scores of homes were carved out what was once a big box store, at least at first. The demand for cheap housing exploded right after the war, and scores of these types of structures were cannibalized. The additions to the building showed hasty construction and low-quality materials. Flaking paint, missing siding panels, and uncut grass sprouted around the miniature courtyard. Despair and desperation resided here.

"Are you sure these are the coordinates?" Fawn looked at Briscoe.

"Yes."

"Why would an AGEH top-tier engineer live in this hole?"

Briscoe eyed the front door to the building's lobby. "He's saving his currency for retirement?"

"Low level security and dodgy surveillance put him

in the higher percentage to be a victim of violators."

"Maybe he was a violator too. I mean, he lived here because he felt comfortable here. Unlike some of these citizens, he *could* afford to live elsewhere."

"It's strange. You'd think they'd insist he move to a more secure location. What if he's poached or eliminated? It happened, anyway—he'd dead—but…" Fawn trailed off as the fact Cho didn't live in a more secure location flabbergasted her.

"Healthy competition?"

"I guess. You got the code to his place?"

"Of course, I do." Briscoe got out of the wauto with a cluck of his tongue in light admonishment.

"Just checking." Fawn laughed.

As they approached the entrance, Briscoe covered his nose with his hand.

"It smells like…"

"…Ackback and grease. Fried tofu?" Fawn coughed out the bitter odor.

"It's strong. Someone's cooking it up fresh."

Fawn grunted in agreement, and she prayed she didn't get another headache from the fumes. They made their way to the fifth floor in the musty elevator car. No one joined them. The creaking cables made Fawn's stomach knot up. Thankfully, they arrived in quick fashion. As soon as the doors slid back, they rushed out in hopes of cleaner air in the corridor.

The hallway bore beige walls with graffiti colorful in both images and languages. It didn't reek. The floor wasn't sticky, which was more than they could say for the sole operating elevator car.

Briscoe lit a cigarette. "I gotta get that smell outta my nose."

"What's the loft number?"

"It's letter G."

Fawn headed left, where the lettered doors appeared to move further along the alphabet. Recessed overhead lighting provided weak illuminated patches. Muffled music seeped out from behind some of the closed doors. Shouts and moans came from another.

"These walls are paper thin." Briscoe blew smoke from his nostrils.

"Here we are—G."

Briscoe punched in the security code. They waited a breath before entering the apartment. Cho's home mimicked his Anderson Clinic workspace. Minimalist style furniture with sleek lines. Various schematics covered sections of the walls.

"You thinking what I'm thinking?" Briscoe glanced at Fawn.

"This place's been rummaged through."

"Exactly."

"What were they looking for?"

"And did they find it?" Fawn stepped further inside.

The door hushed closed.

"It's so quiet here," Briscoe said.

"This unit sits at the end of the hallway."

Briscoe walked over to the gray loveseat. He stepped over discarded cords, wires, and tools. Sunlight came through the open windows. The rain had pushed on.

Fawn spied, from her spot, the doctor's work area, a bathroom, and a kitchenette. To her left, an alcove and another section of the open space was separated by a curtain.

"His work station's basically this entire area." Fawn spread her arms wide.

"Yes, you can see the bot parts in a trail from the table there and back." Briscoe pointed to the stream of items.

At the foot of the loveseat, sat a pair of gray fuzzy slippers.

Such a lonely existence. Fawn pressed her lips together. *Not entirely different from mine.*

A shiver raced down her spine.

Thwack!

Briscoe took out his gun. The tension increased. Then a *thud* made them both jump. Their eyes met.

Someone's in here.

"The hell?" Fawn glanced at Briscoe.

He put his finger to his lips to hush her. She raised her baton and cursed her captain for taking her gun before her actual end date.

They split up. Briscoe took his right side of the room, Fawn took her right side, as they faced each other.

She crept down the short hallway. Her shaky breathing echoed in her ears. Danger lingered along the edge of the robotic parts, wires, plastic storage containers, and random monitors. Within the shadows, there were good places to hide. Some of the containers were stacked as high as she was tall.

"Regulator! Come out with hands high!" Fawn shouted. Damn, her legs shook. She switched the baton to the other hand and took turns wiping her palms on her pants.

This isn't the time to be all jittery.

From behind her, Briscoe shouted. "District regs!"

He sounded far away. Fawn entered what resembled a bedroom. The door was open. A thin gray sheet poured from the bed to the floor. The pungent odors of old sweat and unwashed laundry rolled forward.

Fawn spotted a pile of soiled clothing beside the bed. Here, too, various robots awaited assembly. They circled the bed, a river of debris and unseeing eyes, limbs, and chips. She swept her baton to the right of the entrance and inched toward what could only be described as a small closet. The closet held a few hangers, but no clothes. Apparently, Cho kept them someplace else, perhaps the floor, like the others.

The closet was shaped like a U, with the opening being how she entered. On her left, a section of the wall had recessed drawers. She relaxed, intrigued by curiosity.

No one's here. Maybe he kept stuff in here.

"Clear. Oh, hey, you found something?"

Briscoe's sudden presence made her jump and whirl with her baton raised.

"Whoa! It's me."

"You didn't find anyone?" Fawn lowered her baton and replaced it at her belt.

"No. It's probably rats or raccoons. There's food left out on the kitchen counter."

Fawn shuddered. "BB…"

Briscoe reached over her shoulder. The narrow width only allowed one person inside.

Fawn pressed the top drawer to open it.

Nothing happened.

It lacked a handle. None of the drawers had one.

Fawn squatted down to get a better look. She took out her handheld and switched on the flashlight. "Wait a minute. This is all one unit."

"Fake drawers."

Fawn knocked on the wall around the drawers. "There's something behind here. Look for a release or lever or something to open it."

They retreated from the closet and fanned out across the bedroom.

"He'd keep it close. No way he wanted to lose it in this mess. He hoarded circuits, limbs, chips, wires, motherboards…" Briscoe said.

"If I was Cho, where would I put the release?" Fawn stood at the end of the bed and faced the closet. She scanned the wall for any hint of a secret panel or something indicating a way to open the drawers. She closed her eyes to put herself in Cho's mindset. He kept his work life scattered around his living space. The two melded together.

Fawn sighed. She opened her eyes. "It's gotta be something robot related."

"Or not," Briscoe said as he dug under a flat pillow. "Here."

"What's that?" Fawn came over to him. The thin oval device held raised colored buttons. "Why would he keep a tele-monitor remote under his pillow?"

Briscoe held it up. "The kicker is, there aren't any tele-monitors in this place."

Fawn brightened. "Go on, then. Click it."

"Pressing the big red button now."

Inside the closet, the faux drawers hissed as the unit disappeared into the walls, revealing another room. Fawn and Briscoe walked over to get a closer look. It made her uneasy.

"BB..."

Briscoe removed his ornate coat and handed it to Fawn. He gave her the remote, too. Without looking at her, he rolled up his sweater's sleeves and took his hand-held from his coat's inner pocket.

"I'm going in." He switched on the handheld's flashlight.

"Be careful."

Her heart inched into her throat. If being a regulator had taught her anything in the last five years, it was that danger often lay closer than anyone expected. Leonard Cho didn't expect to get off the cargo craft and be dead before he reached his office.

She watched Briscoe get on his hands and knees, wincing at the dusty floor. With both hands, he crawled forward, the handheld clenched in one fist. His feet disappeared into the gloomy depths.

A crash grabbed her attention. A spray of light and then darkness. She felt nauseous.

"BB! You alright?" She threw the coat on the bed and hurried to the inner closet with a terrible gut feeling. "BB!"

She took a deep breath before getting on her knees and plowing through the same dark entrance-way. Once she cleared the panel, she stood and waited for her eyes to adjust to the gloom. *No light in here. Where's BB's flashlight? BB?*

"BB," she whispered.

Nothing.

Thick quiet blanketed the area, except for a mechanical humming. It permeated the space. She couldn't determine its length or width. Out of the corner of her eye a fluttering green light caught her attention. She swallowed the lump of anxiety blocking her ability to breathe.

"BB?"

All at once, a high-pitched shriek exploded from the dark. A hard *thwack* resounded. Fawn backpedaled toward the doorway. A spray of light lit up the shadows.

Laser-gun fire erupted beside her. The *whirr* of its blast came too close for comfort.

She screamed and froze. Her heart pounded like a cargo train. She crouched down and covered her ears. Her stomach went hollow. Overwhelming indecision paralyzed her. *Run? Stay? Fight? Flee?*

"BB!" she screamed.

A light switched on. "Fawn? You okay?"

Briscoe touched her shoulder. She yelled and scooted further back against the wall as if to disappear into it, before she caught herself.

"BB?"

"It's me. I'm sorry if I startled you." Briscoe had blood smears across his cheek and nose.

Relief washed over her. *He's alive.*

But something about his eyes made her uneasy.

She followed his gaze.

Ahead, lying on its side, a metallic, square-shaped robot with painted facial features shot sparks and sputtered. Circuits and wires shone through the laser-gun hole in its body. Briscoe stood up and—with his gun trained on the bot—went to it.

Fawn waited for the adrenaline to recede. The closet surprised her with an unexpected revelation.

"This is a disturbing discovery."

"You think?" Briscoe said over his shoulder.

"You're bleeding." Fawn pointed at his abdomen.

Briscoe looked down. "I am. I didn't feel it, but now you mention it, it hurts. Guess I was too busy trying not to die when it attacked me."

Fawn stood on shaky legs. "I knew something wasn't right. I had a feeling."

"I bet this is Cho's devious secret project Dr. Baldwin didn't want to tell us about." Briscoe poked the bot with his gun. "It tried to kill me."

"You think Dr. Baldwin knew about this?"

Briscoe put a fresh, unlit cigarette in his mouth. "Maybe. Could be why they didn't move him to a more secure sector. No one's gonna ask questions around here. No one's gonna connect to regulators, either."

"This smaller lab didn't come cheap. We already know Cho's currency account was scrapping bottom. No, this is probably AGEH work. A little room to keep their secret safe in case of a break-in."

Briscoe slid down to the floor and groaned. "I am floating outside my body, Fawn. Tether me!"

"You need help. I'm calling it in."

Briscoe closed his eyes, and didn't respond.

CHAPTER SEVEN

AN HOUR LATER, Briscoe sat on the edge of the victim's bed while medics applied liquid sutures to his wounds. Fawn hovered close to him.

"What the hell is this?" Mario James, lead robotics vioTechnician, said. He stood inside the closet with his mouth agape. He turned his dark eyes to them and adjusted his hand on his processing kit.

"It's exactly what it looks like, a hidden workspace," Fawn said. "A series of clues we need to uncover, James. You should start with the bot and gather as many digital breadcrumbs as you can, as soon as you can."

Briscoe said, "The moment I entered the secret room, the thing attacked. The limbs are blades so be careful. It's been modified."

"You seem okay," Mario said with a glance back at Briscoe.

"My sweater isn't." Briscoe smirked and pointed to the sutures.

"The pain patches are a nice touch," Mario teased.

"I'll show you." Fawn pointed to the entrance.

Mario bent down on his knees and crawled inside, pushing his kit ahead of him. Fawn followed him back inside. With the lights on, the workspace looked less threatening. On two walls paper schematics as well as flowcharts depicted plans for a nurse bot. A square table held an n-bot shell. Its guts spilled out onto the surface. Tools lay scattered around the pool of cords and wires. A three-foot tall lantern sat in the center and provided illumination.

"Let me get started. Come on, Jax! I need your digital expertise." Mario stood and sighed.

Jax's face appeared at the entrance. Her long braids and bright pink lipstick conveyed youth, but she had four grandchildren. She crawled inside the room with her own processing kit and groaned as she took in the space.

"Wow. Secret lair." Jax laughed.

Mario snapped on his latex gloves. "Comic book style."

"This guy lived alone. Right?" Jax looked at Fawn.

"Yes."

"You can always tell. No partner's gonna put up with all this robotic sprawl, so I wonder why he had a hidden room." Jax zipped up her protective suit and took out her black latex gloves.

"We have the same question," Fawn said.

Mario squatted down in front of the damaged robot. Over his shoulder, he said, "This looks like some serious custom work. With luck, the data's stored in the cloud or some offsite server. The blast did a lot of damage."

"Same here!" Briscoe shouted from the entranceway. "Raul loves this sweater."

Fawn rolled her eyes. "Let us know what you find."

"You got it," Jax said.

Fawn hurried out of the workspace. Once she exited the closet, Briscoe came to her and squeezed her shoulder.

"Are you sure you're okay?"

She gave him a weak smile. "Sure. It's you I'm worried about."

"I can replace the sweater…"

"BB, you should go home. Rest. I heard the medic."

He placed an arm over his injury. "I got a few pain patches. I'm good."

He looked pale and sweaty. She retrieved his coat, before guiding him to back to the bed and making him lie down.

"You should go home. Let Raul take care of you. He's a doctor." Fawn brushed his damp bangs aside.

He's hurt because of me.

"I'm sorry I froze in there."

Briscoe said, "These sheets smell like oil and stale sex." He struggled to sit up. "VioTech should take these for analysis."

"Did you hear me?" She crossed her arms.

Briscoe wiped his face. "Yeah. Look, if you'd gone in there first, you could've been killed. You came in and caused a distraction. That gave me time to change positions and fire on the blasted thing. I'm thankful all we got is a few flesh wounds."

He cleared his throat and groaned when he involuntarily moved. "Get vioTech in here."

"You should take leave, IR Baker," Dr. Rycroft walked in the bedroom, followed by two white-clad techs with their own processing kits. "Take the sheets and process this room, though both IRs have ruined some of it. Get what you can."

Briscoe stood up with a grunt. "Sorry, doctor, trying to survive. We couldn't think about your violation scene, but definitely grab those sheets."

Dr. Rycroft didn't smile. "Stab wounds to the abdomen heal slowly."

"Yeah. Okay. The doctor told me."

"So did I, and the medics," Fawn said.

"It's nice to get all this attention…"

"BB!" She guided him into the larger living space. Once out of earshot, she said, "Who was Cho getting busy with?"

"Dunno."

Briscoe ran a hand through his hair before bending over and resting his hands on his knees. The adrenaline had dropped. She recognized the system withdrawal systems. He was visibly shaking.

"Let's go. I'm flying." Fawn threw his coat around his shoulders.

Briscoe slowly followed; his almond-shaped eyes glossed over.

Her heart pinched. *The pain patches must not be enough to battle back the pain. Each breath must cause some agony.*

She took his hand to lead and reassure him.

Or maybe it was the other way around.

Briscoe squeezed her hand.

They'd have to wait for robotics to conduct their investigation and conclude their findings. Mario would send her a robotic autopsy report. She had time to get Briscoe home.

Once in the pilot's seat, she checked Briscoe's safety belt before launching the flight sequence. Her partner reclined his seat as far as it could go before closing his eyes. His ornate coat covered him like a blanket. He remained pale beneath his usual tan skin tone.

They entered the elevated lanes, and Fawn set the autopilot. It took over when she finished entering Briscoe's address.

"I'm connecting to Raul. You shouldn't be home alone." Fawn pressed the tele-monitor button.

"He's working," Briscoe whispered.

"Contact Raul."

In seconds, Raul—with mask and head covering—appeared on screen.

"BB? What's happened?" Raul's dark eyes darted as he tried to see everything. "Fawn? Where's BB?"

"He's here beside me. We're on the way to your house."

"Why? What's happened?" Raul snatched his mask away from his mouth.

Fawn hesitated. Raul didn't need the details of their violation scene, but she had to tell him something. Panic raised his voice an octave. This was probably his worst nightmare made real.

"First, BB's fine. Medics applied liquid sutures, pain patches with nano-antibotics..."

"Bloody hell! He's not fine, Fawn, if he needed stitches. You're flying him home, meaning he can't fly himself. Is he conscious?"

"He's resting. We were searching the victim's flat when we were ambushed." Fawn's face burned and her voice shook.

Raul seethed. "And only BB got hurt? No doubt trying to save your ass. You're a liability."

"We didn't see it coming." Fawn swallowed the embarrassment lodged in her throat.

"You never do!" Raul shouted.

His anger caused her to break out in a sweat. Her hands became fists. She glanced at Briscoe, then back to Raul's furious and pinched face. She punched her thigh.

I should've done more!

Her failings could've gotten her partner killed, and it *had* caused him injury.

"Raul, he shouldn't be alone. Is there someone to stay with him?"

"We have an n-bot. That'll do until I can get there." Raul disconnected.

Fawn fell back in the pilot's seat with a soft thud. She took a deep steadying breath. Briscoe opened his eyes as if he'd heard her fear.

"He's worried." Briscoe lids lowered again.

"He isn't the only one."

CHAPTER EIGHT

FAWN CLIMBED out of the taxi and into the chilly afternoon breeze outside Regulator Headquarters. She'd left Briscoe nestled in his favorite chaise, covered with a blanket, and a hovering n-bot. Once she'd confirmed he was comfortable, she bolted. She didn't want to run into Raul. The shame reached out to her.

Take some deep breaths.

She did as her inner coach suggested as she headed into the building.

With her head bowed and her collar up, she hurried through the lower level. When she entered the second floor, investigators turned their heads to look at her. Great. The other regs murmured as she passed. News of the fiasco at Cho's loft had arrived before she did. The tips of her ears burned, but she didn't engage with anyone. Instead, she power-walked to her office.

"You don't look too good, Granger."

Fawn hung her coat on its hook before turning to face Neese.

"Are you stalking me?"

Neese rolled his eyes. His facial tattoo blinked. He wore his usual expensive inspector clothes, designer jeans, green sweater, and boots. His identification swung from his neck on a chain, but Fawn wore hers pinned to her coat.

"No."

"That's exactly what a stalker would say," Fawn said as she went to her desk. *If I pretend, he isn't here, he will leave.*

"I heard about Baker, but I've confirmed Damoni Brees's whereabouts." Neese beamed.

"You're still here?"

Neese said, "Yeah. Tom lured her to a location so we gotta move to capture her."

"Lured her? With what? Why?" Fawn stood up again.

"You should come with us to pick her up."

"Why?" Fawn repeated.

"One last flight before you hang it all up," Neese said.

"Sure." She retrieved her coat.

Neese led her out of the office. "I'll explain more as we go."

Fawn frowned. Neese was only ever concerned about having his own way. Something didn't sit well with her. He had a strange note in his voice.

Her gut burned in warning. Neese never did anything that didn't benefit him.

She followed him down the stairwell and out to the

regulator vehicle yard. Doing anything with Neese was out of character, but she wanted to find the link between Cho and Damoni, if one existed. Neese believed there was, but she wasn't sure.

A cargo craft flew over to them, blowing debris and hot air, not unlike Neese. The side door rose, revealing Inspector Regulator Daniel Tom, Neese's current partner. He waved.

"Get in!"

He reached out to Neese to help him in. The cargo craft almost drowned him out. He wore sunglasses and a one-piece navy regulator uniform. Neese stepped on to the liftbar and grabbed the overhead handle to pull himself inside. He clasped Daniel on the shoulder before disappearing into the dim interior.

With a gloved hand outstretched in her direction, Daniel shouted, "You coming?"

"Sure!" Fawn grabbed his hand and hauled herself into the vehicle in a spur of the moment decision.

Inside, she found an empty seat between two more uniformed regulators. Bucket seats lined the driver's side of the craft, and three adjacent seats took up the back. They faced the driver, while the side seats pointed in the direction of the vehicle's side door. One seat was on either side of the side door-panel. The regulators nodded in greeting.

The door whined as Daniel closed it.

Fawn secured her safety harness and let her eyes adjust to the dim interior.

"I'm IR Daniel Tom, Neese's partner. I think we've met before."

"Didn't you used to work patrol?"

Daniel smiled. "Didn't we all?"

Fawn inclined her head. *Touché.*

He sat across from Neese. Both men smiled at each other. Another regulator flew, while someone sat in the front passenger seat as they lunged gently forward and up into the elevated lanes.

In all, six regulators, plus her. "Why so many of us, Neese? Three more and a few guns and we're a field commando unit."

Daniel raised his sunglasses. He had beautiful, piercing hazel eyes.

"She's suspicious of me."

"Who, Granger?" Neese jutted his thumb at her.

"No, Damoni," Daniel said. "For context, IR Granger, I've been undercover for the last six months, attempting to infiltrate the Human Rights League's hacker team. Those individuals are scattered across territories, as you can imagine, but I managed to befriend Damoni."

Neese said, "It's been very difficult to track her whereabouts."

"She met me in a café a few weeks ago, and all hell broke out. An altercation occurred between her and my associates. Foul play was involved, and my cover was blown. When we tried to detain her, she went to ground. It's taken weeks to find her again. I don't want to take a chance and lose her."

"Do we know for sure she's at this location?" Fawn said.

"There have been door checks and surveillance. Digital evidence doesn't lie," Daniel said.

"No, but it can be manipulated," Fawn said.

Daniel's pinched expression hinted at his confusion. He turned away from her and spoke softly and friendly to one of the regulators seated up front.

"What does she know or have?" Fawn said to Neese.

His amused face became stoic while Daniel bit his lip. They both avoided eye contact with her.

Fawn crossed her arms. "Well?" She glanced from one to the other. She lingered on Daniel.

And he immediately caved.

"Among other info, like the intel on Dr. Cho, Damoni has our list of confidential informants," Daniel said. He rubbed his hands together. "If she publishes it, people will die."

"That's alarming information. I haven't heard anything about it," Fawn said.

"We've kept it hushed for obvious reasons," Daniel said.

"You know what happens to snitches, right, Granger?" Neese checked his laser-gun.

A pit formed in the bottom of her stomach. *Snitches get stitches*. It was an old urban saying to dissuade people from working with regulators. "Yeah, but how did she get a secure HQ file?"

Neese swore. "We've said enough already. We've hashed everything. Just focus on your own violation. You're here to observe."

She saw right through his façade. He wanted to control the story, and the flow of information too. *He's nervous, but why?*

"Do you have any leverage? Why do you suspect she

wouldn't she keep mum?" Fawn watched Daniel, but he wore his poker face.

And a tiny smirk.

Neese popped up. "Leave it to *us*."

He composed himself, adjusting his sweater, checking his shoes, and his slacks. Fidgeting. He was distraught.

Across from him, Daniel didn't say anything more. He just hummed.

Taking the hint, Fawn settled into the flight to Sector 6. The sooner she solved Cho's death violation, the better she'd feel. The idea of leaving it incomplete for Briscoe to solve on his own, didn't sit well with her.

What crucial piece of evidence did Damoni hold? Information on Cho? On AGEH?

She shook off the pensive thoughts.

She had no way to know what Damoni knew or if she'd even speak to them. The uneasy feeling remained a knot in her stomach. So, she observed the changing scenes outside the craft's oblong windows. Briscoe's weakened state lingered in the back of her mind, a thin ghost a glimpse out-of-view.

Raul was right. She *was* a liability, and not three hours after she'd gotten BB hurt, she'd set off on another gut hunch. Would she put these regs in danger too? She closed her eyes to push back against the rising anxiety threatening to envelope her.

To regain her focus, Fawn deleted the noise and the uncertainties—at least for now.

"Sorry to hear about IR Baker," Daniel's husky voice infiltrated Fawn's Zen attempt.

She looked at him. Apparently, everyone had heard

about the botched Cho search, but Daniel appeared sincere.

"He's not dead," Fawn said.

"No, but multiple stabs to the trunk hurt." Daniel raised his eyebrows as if envisioning the pain.

"Two..."

"Two?" Daniel frowned.

"Yeah. Briscoe received two stab wounds."

"I said multiple, and that includes two. Right?"

"Two is a couple. BB got a couple of stab wounds. Multiple makes it sound like he was knifed 40 times." Fawn sighed. She didn't want the narrative to get any more outrageous or exaggerated.

Daniel's incredulous expression made Neese's sour face break into a grin.

"He'll be okay." Fawn wanted to shrink between the two regs and into the upholstery.

"Oh, yeah, but probably not before Friday," Neese said.

Daniel caught Neese's jeering tone. "Okay, I'll bite. Do I even want to know? What's Friday?"

"My last day."

"Wow. You don't look old enough to retire..."

Neese snorted. The other regulators broke out in laughter.

A dumbfounded Daniel sat with a what-the-hell look on his face. "Well, she doesn't."

"Thank you, but I'm not retiring, just relocating," Fawn said. The laughter forced her to say *something* but just enough. "It's complicated, IR Tom."

"Isn't it always with you, Granger?"

"Death's messy, Neese." Fawn folded her hands in her lap to keep from punching him.

Daniel caught the finality in her voice. "Right. I wish IR Baker a speedy recovery. He's a good person."

And I don't deserve him. Right, IR Tom? It didn't surprise her. Over the past five years, one IR or another had commented on all the ways she lacked compared to Briscoe. Hell, even Captain Brinnington, after the *incident,* told her he only kept her on because of her partner. They tried to pin their mistakes on her.

She didn't believe any of them.

They kept her as an IR because she was damn good at it. It made the others nervous, but it didn't bother Briscoe.

Neese sobered as the craft veered left, then lowered.

The flash of a big arc light followed by clanking and crunching metal silenced the craft. It sent chills down her spine. Her heart pounded against her chest, but in slow thumps. The regs beside her remained quiet and still.

Neese unbuckled his harness.

"We're here."

CHAPTER NINE

"WHERE'S HERE?" Fawn unbuckled her safety harness in concert with the other regulators.

Outside the sky looked unremarkable and unfamiliar. She didn't get out to Sector 8 often. She rose to get a better view through the window.

"Is that a factory?" She looked over to Daniel.

He lowered his sunglasses to cover his eyes. "We're about a block outside the target area. The rest of the way, we go on foot."

The regulators got up and began checking their gear, pulling on laser-proof vests and helmets. The pilot lowered a tele-monitor from the ceiling and the outside landscape appeared.

"We're dealing with people who have nothing left to lose," Neese said to Daniel.The regulator seated in the passenger seat said, "Sending out the drone shortly, sir."

Neese said, "Ado and Farris, canvas the block around the contact point. Stay alert. She's probably not alone."

To Fawn he said, "Stay here. We'll contact you once we get her."

Fawn nodded, though she didn't like it. One glance at her baton told her she wouldn't be any good if it turned violent like the last time. She remained seated while Daniel opened the side panel. The metal screamed as he did so.

"As you know, the intended target is Damoni Brees. She's clearly dangerous. Let's go up the ante!" Neese shouted.

Clearly, they liked the game of hide and seek with the violator. There were smiles and nervous chuckles. Fawn found the variables too dangerous for it to be a game.

They filed out of the cargo craft and into the barren section of the sector. Discarded tires littered the area outside what appeared to be a factory. The team fanned out, dark beetles across hot asphalt.

Fawn got out of the craft. From behind the hatch, one of the regulators reappeared. She carried a silver painted drone in one hand and its controller in the other. Only the two of them remained, so Fawn approached her.

"I'm IR Fawn Granger."

"I'm Regulator Puco," she said.

Puco had a close-cropped haircut and large, round brown eyes. A heart-shaped face and a robust frame made her appear young.

"I've got to get this bird in the air, okay?" Puco said.

"Right." Fawn followed her back into the cargo craft.

Puco plopped down into the passenger seat, spun it around to face the ceiling-dropped tele-monitor. Her nimble fingers flew across the controller's buttons as her eyes remained glued to the screen. The cameras switched from the craft's to the drone's in seconds. The tele-monitor flickered and then became steady.

The drone's buzz grew faint as it flew out the door and away, in the direction of the regulator team. The tele-monitor view provided eye-opening shots of the factory and the grounds. Puco flew with an easy elegance.

"What do you see?" Neese's question came through the craft's internal speakers.

"Nothing so far," Puco said.

"Where is everyone?" Fawn whispered.

"I don't know."

"That's not encouraging." Fawn peered at the screen.

The drone soared around the factory, but none of the regulators appeared on screen. Large swaths of paved lots and sidewalks didn't leave many hiding places for coverage.

"They must be inside already," Puco said.

Then, just out-of-frame, a regulator appeared outside the abandoned dock with a weapon drawn. As the drone came closer, shouting erupted from inside. The noise snared Fawn's attention, but on screen the sole regulator crept quickly forward to the dock's opening.

"Who's that?" Fawn pointed at the tele-monitor.

"I think that's Ado." Puco's response wasn't normal.

She should be anxious, but there was nothing but cold calm. *Does the young regulator lack empathy or awareness of how serious this situation is?*

Hell, maybe I do.

"Why is Ado alone? Where are the others? Who shouted and why is it suddenly so damn quiet? This is bizarre." Fawn started for the factory with her baton in her fist.

Was Neese attempting to conceal evidence? Maybe it was the PTSD from *the incident* with Neese, but Fawn walked faster to get to the factory.

Ado had already disappeared into the open dimness.

Fawn followed their path, scrambling through the dock bay's partially opened door.

And right into a fight.

"Granger, watch out!" Daniel shouted, seconds before a laser-gun blast zipped by Fawn's face.

She immediately scurried for cover behind what was once sorting machinery with her heart fluttering. Her blood roared in her ears, her knees burned from sliding across the floor on them, and her left elbow ached from landing on it. When she peeked out to see what was happening, people's mouths moved, but she couldn't hear anything.

A short distance away from her, in the middle of the open warehouse, one of the regulators lay sprawled on their back. Bruising on their face hid their identity from this distance.

Who delivered that brutal beating?

Through watering eyes, Fawn spied Daniel's and Neese's positions behind two overturned machines. Like hers, their metal-sorting apparatus had mechanical hands that looked like claws, and a rubber-like conveyor belt.

The place smelled like oil and age. Rust covered some of the machines and coated most surfaces with its reddish-orange dust. She didn't see anyone who wasn't dressed in regulator clothing, so where was Damoni and her crew?

"Come on, Damoni! You've done enough," Daniel said. He took advantage of a pause in gun blasts. "This type of violence isn't you."

"Go delete yourself!" The disgust in Damoni's voice made her sound monstrous.

And a bit inhuman.

A voice modifier?

"Let's talk. That's all we want…all *I* want," Daniel said.

He's good. Fawn shook her head as she lowered herself back behind the machine's protection. He'd nearly convinced her he cared about Damoni. No doubt he utilized the undercover persona to appeal to her emotions and their relationship. It was genius.

Too bad we couldn't apply it to human ones.

"You want me to do some casual labor for The District?" Damoni sounded closer than before. "Like you said."

"¡*Si*! Look, I'm putting down my weapon."

A breathtaking claim, and—to Fawn's horror—Daniel slowly stood up and placed his laser-gun on the floor in front of him. He looked left and right in search of Damoni. His warm tone acted a perfect lure.

"I see, but the rest of your squad didn't," Damoni said as she lowered herself from a hole in the ceiling via illuminated hover-board. She held a blaster in both hands. A black backpack was strapped to her torso, and she wore a laser-proof vest of her own. Safety goggles protected her eyes and a thin microphone lead ran from her right ear to her mouth. She wore all black clothing and thick-soled boots. Each piece of her clothing hugged her curves. She wore her age with the confidence of a wise woman who'd lived a life and knew all of its secrets. It shined in her tone, and her even-faster reflexes. Lithe, limber, she moved like a much younger person.

Fawn let out a quiet "Wow."

Somehow, Damoni had rigged speakers throughout the space and when she spoke, everyone heard.

Had Daniel been foolish enough to let her pick the rendezvous spot?

Neese eased himself to his feet with his laser-gun trained on Damoni. Daniel remained empty-handed, but his weapon was within reach. Two other regulators emerged a bit from their coverage areas.

But when Fawn counted, there were more regulators than they had arrived with.

Now she knew where Damoni's people were located.

Fawn scuttled closer to Daniel and Neese's location. Gaps in coverage prevented her from reaching them. A numbness spilled over her.

Sirens wailed, making them all jump.

Puco's voice erupted from the craft's PA system. "Damoni Brees, come out with your hands up."

Damoni's head jerked up from peering down at them as she hovered above. She grinned. She reached inside her backpack and retrieved something. The glint from the item cast a flickering warning seconds before a high whistle pierced the room.

Fawn shot to her feet. "Flash bang!"

An explosion of light burst through the warehouse.

A sharp, burning pain flared in Briscoe's abdomen, jolting him from a fitful slumber. The recliner careened left, but Raul snatched the arm before Briscoe toppled to their wooden floor.

"Whoa!"

"Argh!"

"Your pain patches must've worn off while you were asleep. You've done nothing but grunt and toss and turn." Raul patted his arm and straightened the blanket over his lap again. He placed a hand against Briscoe's damp forehead. "Still no fever. Good."

Briscoe groaned as he wiped sleep from his eyes and hoisted himself to a sitting position. He raised the recliner enough to be at an angle, but upright enough to see the room.

"Here. Drink this."

"Is it sake?" Briscoe accepted the teacup.

"Sythtea. No alcohol until after you're all healed. Plus, too much of it will cause gut rot."

Briscoe stilled at Raul's doctor tone. Normally, he left that at work where a fast, direct, and emotionless voice helped avoid confusion, kept everyone on task—but in their home, they curated love, acceptance, and support. Briscoe closed his eyes and recalled the biting terror in Raul's conversation with Fawn on the flight home. It came out like anger to her.

"I'm gonna get more patches," Raul said.

Oh, he is *pissed.*

As Raul swept by him, Briscoe grabbed his arm,

halting him from moving on. The tremor surprised him. Raul wasn't angry so much as he was *scared.* For an Emergency Room doctor to be frightened at his injuries woke Briscoe all the way up.

"Come here. Stop. Please," Briscoe winced at the soreness, but fought not to show it.

Raul turned and knelt by Briscoe's recliner. Briscoe tugged Raul down, enveloping him despite the awkward recliner between them.

"I'm okay," Briscoe whispered against his hair.

"If I'd lost you…"

"…but you didn't." Briscoe clasped Raul tighter as warm tears wet his neck.

Briscoe rubbed his hair and let his partner fall into him, to be present in the moment, to turn away from the terrifying, potential future. They existed in the now, flawed but together, their love a buoy in the vast, inky ocean of uncertainty comprising The District.

When Raul pulled back, he said, "Tell me what happened. Fawn flaked out, didn't she?"

Briscoe adjusted his position and cursed at the desire to be comfortable while knowing it was his own body causing the discomfort—and he couldn't escape it.

"Well, we were ambushed. You know Fawn's last day is Friday, so the captain took her weapon. We went to the victim's home to look for clues, just doing our job. It was deemed safe and clear. There wasn't forced entry or anything indicating a danger existed at the site. I went in first because I had a gun. She only had a field baton."

"He left her with only a field baton? That's troubling."

"Yeah. Damn him."

"You need a new partner."

"Going to happen soon, love."

"When's her last day?"

"Friday. Like I said."

"Can't some soon enough. For some, the psychological injuries never heal. A scar remains and demands to be scratched from time to time." Raul stood, wiping his face to clear the tears.

He took Briscoe's right hand and applied two pain patches. "I had these in my pocket. I already changed your sutures. The wounds aren't too deep."

"I told you I was fine." Briscoe cleared his throat, but kept his head bowed.

"You should be able to move around once the pain patches' nanos get to work. I gave you both a pain management one and a booster to speed up healing." Raul kissed his forehead. "You hungry?"

"Yes." Briscoe picked up his tea and sipped.

Raul headed into the kitchen.

Briscoe found his tele-monitor and scrolled, looking for any missed messages.

None from Fawn.

Where are you?

He sighed and attempted to connect with her. *I hope she's not still blaming herself.*

Sometimes, when Fawn fell into the cavern of guilt and self-doubt, she wandered so far in, she lost herself in misery and despair.

"You haven't reached Granger. Leave a message."

"It's me. You aren't napping on this death vio. Are

you? We're not close to finding who did this. Are you there stirring the pot? Connect to me."

Urgency pressed and nagged at him. He sipped the lukewarm tea, taking bigger gulps now it had cooled somewhat. He sighed. The emotional turmoil the case was racking up must have threatened Fawn's condition. The anxiety would build and then explode, rendering her to her knees and then to her bed.

The banging of pots and pans erupted from the kitchen. The roar of water and the refrigerator door's annoyed *ding, ding* spoke to Raul's prep. Briscoe's hunger awoke and growled in complaint.

He went to his tablet. Perhaps the reports had come in. Maybe he could delve into new clues. There could be news from the re-canvas.

Anything!

Raul came in from the kitchen. "You're restless already. Did I hear you talking to someone?"

"Running down leads."

"You're supposed to rest."

"I know but this death violation was a devious, intentional killing."

"Every death vio is important. As your partner and physician I'm confiscating these items so you can rest."

"Wait! No!"

"Doctor's orders."

Raul wrestled the tele-monitor from Briscoe's sweaty hands. He snatched the tablet before Briscoe could intercept.

"No fair! Taking advantage of the wounded." Briscoe yelled to a fleeing Raul.

The nurse bot came to life, floating out of its corner charging pad.

"You are wounded. Do you require assistance?"

Briscoe bristled at the painted, glowing smile. The male voice held just enough human programmed notes to be disarming—if you weren't looking at it.

"No."

"I detect injury."

"I'm fine. Go!" Briscoe waved it off. *Insistent damn thing.*

He laid back in the chair, reclined again to ease the pressure. The stabbing wasn't deep and Raul enjoyed taking care of him.

A soft *whirring* drew his attention. The electrical crackling raised the hair on his arms. The nurse bot remained at his side, smiling, waiting to administer aid, to be useful, to help.

Briscoe frowned. He *was* hurt but didn't require assistance.

And he'd dismissed it.

Why is it still there?

"Ra?"

"Yeah?"

"Is there a special code to power down the n-bot?"

Instead of an answer, the sizzle and hiss of cooking emerged with delicious aromas. Minutes passed before Raul appeared at the threshold between the kitchen and dining room, wiping his hands on a towel, his exposed forehead damp with perspiration.

"Sorry. What?"

Briscoe pointed at the nurse bot and repeated his question.

Raul frowned at the egg-shaped robot. "Weird. Once you answer the assistance question, they're supposed to return home. Reboot it. Manually powering it down should fix it. It probably just needs an update or something. Then come eat."

"Okay."

Briscoe eased himself into a sitting position and then to a standing position. His belly burned as injured muscles pulled taut to support his core. Already the meds had eased some of the discomfort enough for him to be on his feet.

He approached the still hovering nurse bot and pressed the OFF button on the left side panel. Its control panel flickered then lit up in red—as if furious—as it returned to its charging pad before falling dark.

As Briscoe headed gingerly to the kitchen, it occurred to him the nurse bot was the same height and shape as the one that had stabbed him.

He froze.

A chill hurried down his spine. The bot hummed as Briscoe watched it from the corner of his eye. The eerie feel of being tracked made his skin crawl.

"Babe!" Raul called from inside the kitchen's warm glow.

"Yeah. Coming."

CHAPTER TEN

"I DIDN'T EXPECT anyone to be alive." Fawn choked on the arid, bitter air. She was shaken.

She was facedown, in a fetal position. The shouts plugged her back in to the current situation. Her ears rang as she rose to her knees. With determination, she held onto the sorting machinery to keep from sliding back down to the dusty floor. If she let her adrenaline take control, she'd make a bad decision.

It felt like forever, but only a few minutes had passed.

Damoni had picked this discreet location to her advantage.

So had Neese and Daniel Tom.

Advantage.

Neese and Daniel staggered into the center, where Damoni lay sprawled, her hands mangled and bloodied. Despite this she got to her feet with a cold sneer of defiance.

"Better make your peace with the creator," Damoni said.

"Don't be mad you got caught," Neese grabbed her wrists and placed blockers on both her wrists. She didn't wince at his rough handling of her injured hands and wrists, but she stared stoically ahead at the exit.

"Are you happy now?" Damoni shouted, breaking her somber expression. "You ought to be deleted!"

Neese lacked empathy. His rough manner caused an exchange of looks from some of the other regulators. Fawn understood the constant scrutiny regulators received from the public. Neese didn't care. He'd check every horrible regulator stereotype box on the list.

On purpose.

"It's done." Daniel raised his protective googles as he made his way to Damoni.

Neese didn't move.

The other regulators looked everywhere but at the two inspectors. They knew it was bad.

"Enough," Daniel softly placed himself between Neese and Damoni. "Come on, Moni."

"You don't call me that. Not anymore." Damoni cut her eyes to Daniel.

He checked her hands before guiding her out with the others of her band remaining. Neese gathered the additional regulators. Fawn struggled to stand.

"What the hell, Neese?"

Neese ignored her. They marched outside the abandoned warehouse to find Puco had relocated the cargo craft to their location.

Damoni and her cohorts punched and kicked in attempts to flee and escape.

Fawn walked out last. Blue and red lights doused them as they made their way from the warehouse. The patrol lights painted everything in the area. Responding regulators reinforced the beam.

Medics arrived and hurried inside to the injured regulator and hurt members of Damoni's crew. Her people all wore reg uniforms.

How did she secure those?

First, how did Damoni get the informant list and now the uniforms? No doubt Damoni was resourceful, but it bothered Fawn.

Why is Neese so eager to incite her to anger?

Did he mean to provoke Damoni so he could kill her? He had a wild look in his eyes before he threw the flash-bang.

He wouldn't be the first to commit a death violation under the guise of upholding regulations.

"Ma'am? Are you alright?" A medic shook her arm. "Inspector?"

Fawn blinked. The medic's smooth, dark face held concern. Deep hazel eyes met Fawn's. Her stomach flopped and her ears burned. The medic's name badge read "Torey."

"You're bleeding." Torey's fingertips brushed the scratches on Fawn's forearms. "Let's get these bandaged up."

"Sure."

Fawn scanned the area for the others. It seemed Puco

had called in backup for the situation. Parked on the pavement at the warehouse were two more cargo crafts, two medical vehicles and several regulator wautos. People were everywhere. She had lost sight of Damoni and Daniel.

Neese found her.

He charged up the small incline to where Fawn and Torey stood.

Once he reached them, he pointed his finger at her. "Next time I tell you to stay put, do it!"

Torey gave him the once-over before returning to applying bandages to Fawn's wounds.

"I don't report to you. Remember? Besides, this was hardly a well-hashed plan."

Neese grinned, but it disappeared as fast as it appeared.

"If you spent any time on patrol, you'd know how situations can get out of control very quickly."

Fawn didn't bother pursuing a debate. Now he knew she understood he'd botched the capture. Yes, he got Damoni, but Ado had been severely beaten before they contained Damoni's associates.

"Where's Damoni? You said I could talk to her." Fawn flexed her arm to show the medic she was fine.

"Report to the infirmary if you discover further injuries later on. And take some time to rest and heal. Not all injuries are physical."

"Thank you, Torey. I will." Fawn avoided eye contact. The pretty medic patted her shoulder and warmth spilled from her touch throughout Fawn's body.

"Promise?" Torey bent a little to catch Fawn's attention.

"Yes, of course." Fawn touched her burning cheeks and glanced up at Torey.

"Good."

"Look, Damoni's not talking to anyone. She's a bit miffed. Daniel's in with her. He may be able to get her to open up," Neese interrupted the tense atmosphere brewing between Fawn and Torey.

"After all his betrayals, I doubt she'll tell him anything." Fawn snorted. "He'll be lucky if she gives him her citizen number."

Neese crossed his arms. "Daniel is good. He'll get it."

"Uh huh. What about Ado's condition? He good too?"

Neese shrugged and rubbed the stubble along his chin.

Fawn sighed.

She'd wasted too much time here. None of this brought her any closer to Cho's violator.

"I'm here, so I'm going to talk to Damoni. Which vehicle is she in?" Fawn dusted off her pants and started for the parked crafts.

Neese rolled his eyes but didn't move. "Fine! If she's refusing to say anything, and you push her, you might get lies. Damoni has no barometer for truth."

Fawn stopped and turned back to Neese. "Which is it? She's a solid source for information or she's a liar? Enough games. The truth, Neese. Now!"

Her volume drew curious looks and others' attention. Some conversations stopped. Others continued albeit lower in tones.

Neese's thick eyebrows shot in the air, and he started walking toward her, a short distance away.

"Truth? I already told you…"

"No. You gave a sliver of the story. Tell me everything. The real reason I'm here. I'm done with this manipulation." Fawn huffed.

The absolute nerve of the man. Why drag her down here then block her access to the source? Neese had something else going on and she didn't need an inspector to see it. She had three more days to resolve Cho's death violation, but Neese's behavior was troubling.

She had no leverage and they both knew it.

Still, she decided to test him and his integrity.

Maybe Neese had become more black-and-white, less gray when it came to morality.

"No one will touch you after the stunt you pulled today. You almost cost me— again. You better hope Ado recovers well. I'm doing you a favor," Neese pushed by her, slamming into her shoulder like a juvenile.

"None of this is my fault! So, keep telling yourself those lies, Neese," Fawn shouted after him.

Neese remained a treacherous ass. No doubt the narrative he'd push with everyone would feature her as the antagonist.

She headed to the newly-arrived crafts. Both had been outfitted to contain violators. She approached the first one on her left. The dark-painted vehicle bore the Regulator logo along with its serial number. A burly man held a laser-gun in one hand, at his side. He had close-cropped purple hair and facial tattoos along the expanse of his forehead. Bright brown eyes gazed down at her over a nose too often broken.

"Inspector?"

"Terry. I need to speak to Damoni Brees. She in there?"

Terry stepped aside and chuckled. "She ain't saying much. She sent Inspector Regulator Tom out of here with his tail between his legs."

"Can't say I blame her."

Fawn stepped up into the cargo craft. In the pilot's seat, a regulator with a short ponytail ran what looked like diagnostics. The empty passenger seat was probably for Terry. No Daniel Tom—maybe he went to see about the others in her group. They might be more cooperative than Damoni. It smelled like disappointment and cigarettes in the tight space.

Behind the passenger seat, Damoni Brees and two of her cohorts sat locked into their individual seats. The bucket seats held neck restraints. It forced the violator to face forward, with limited movement from side to side. They couldn't turn to the left or right due to the blockers. On their wrists, another blocker kept their hands apart. The person could bend their elbows, but they wouldn't be able to maneuver their hands and wrists. A leather strap around their waist pinned them to the seat. Blockers on the ankles kept them from kicking or striking out.

Immobilized. No one spoke.

All three of the violators had a vacant seat between them. Usually, a regulator sat in those seats.

Fawn approached. She would rather do the questioning at headquarters, but, well, here would have to do. She'd lost too much time.

"I'm Inspector Regulator Fawn Granger."

Nothing. Not even a twitch.

"Damoni, I'm here to ask some questions about Dr. Leonard Cho. I'm told you know him."

The name didn't register on Damoni's face.

But her index finger wiggled. A spasm or recognition?

"What can you tell me about him?" Fawn crouched down to be eye level with Damoni, but kept herself an arm's length away.

Damoni's hands bore white gauze and pain patches as they poked out of the blocker. Tear stains decorated her cheeks, and dried blood and scratches lined her forehead and nose.

Her dreadlocked hair remained in its bun, though a few shorter locks escaped and framed her furious, watery eyes. Fawn knew the expression well. It happened to many—mostly women—when overwhelming fury caused them to tear up. They literally burned inside so hotly that their eyes watered.

"He's dead." Fawn watched her.

Damoni looked at her. No tears fell. Only suspicion loomed in those sharp eyes.

"You're lying."

"You know I wouldn't be here if he was still alive."

Damoni licked her full lips and rolled her eyes.

"I'm investigating his death violation. How did you know him?"

Fawn kept her attention on Damoni but noticed it

appeared the entire craft was listening. The AGEH had ears everywhere or so the urban rumors went.

"I know little. Never met the man." Damoni swallowed and looked away.

"Right. Seems I was misinformed." Fawn stood up. "Thank you for your time."

Fawn had taken one step outside when Damoni said, "I said I never met him, not that I didn't *know* him."

Fawn returned to the craft. She sat in the passenger seat and turned it around to face the violator's profile. It forced Damoni to look out the corner of her eyes if she wanted to see Fawn. Not that she bothered.

"What do you know about him?"

"He was a robotics engineer, his specialty nurse bots. I'm betting you already knew that too. What you didn't know was the good engineer loved his bots…in every way."

Fawn leaned in. "Just so I'm clear—you're saying he had a robot addiction?"

"Oh yeah. You're being polite about it. He had a severe case. Drives full of images, videos, and yeah. It got him suspended twice from the AGEH. They scrubbed whatever got leaked online, but the net's sticky. Bits still cling to certain corners, if you know where to look."

"And you know where to look."

Damoni smiled. "Yeah and more, but I ain't saying another damn word until you're ready to deal. Ain't nuthin' free." Her luminous eyes flickered to Fawn.

"Understood." Fawn inched out of the craft.

When Fawn exited the vehicle, she spied Daniel

crossing the pavement, heading in her direction.

"Ah, you've met Damoni then."

"I have. She's a scorpion." Fawn smiled because Daniel's easygoing manner, even when the operation went sideways, was infectious.

"She's something. Imma get her to headquarters and hopefully the flight relaxes her." Daniel winked. "See you."

As Daniel climbed into the cargo craft, Fawn realized Neese's vehicle had already left, along with a few of the other Regulators and medics.

She threw back her head and swallowed the scream growing there.

"Hey, Inspector. You okay?"

Fawn turned to the velvety-voice's owner—Torey.

Not all of the medics had left.

"I'm fine. I'm gonna call an Uber." Fawn shrugged as if them abandoning her didn't make her feel furious and like a complete failure. "Your team heading out?"

Torey nodded and, with a small grin, said, "We got room in the back for you. You heading to Regulator HQ?"

"Yeah." Butterflies erupted in her belly, but Fawn managed to keep them from escaping in a series of giggles. She cleared her throat. "I'd appreciate the ride."

"Sure thing. We're in the big blue right there." Torey pointed to the medical cargo craft painted dark blue with a white stripe around its middle, like a belt. "Jax won't bite, and the injured patient decided he could walk it off. It's just Jax and me, and now, you."

"Perfect." Fawn meant it.

CHAPTER ELEVEN

WEDNESDAY MORNING ARRIVED bright and early with clear skies and a promise of cool temperatures and winds. Briscoe adjusted his coat's collar as he ran up the stairs to the second floor. He stepped through the door with a wheeze and a sharp pang in his stomach. With a mental note to cut back on smoking, he headed to his office, and entered to find Fawn's desk empty. It didn't appear anything had changed since he left yesterday, and he didn't have any connects from his partner.

He removed his coat, hung it, and then walked back out the door.

Where are you, Fawn?

He'd gotten as far as the IR break-room door when he spied her exiting the second-floor stairwell. Their shared office was close to the IR break-room. With her head bent low, she hurried to their shared office without a glance. She disappeared into the space.

Briscoe released a breath he didn't realize he'd been holding until then.

A sinking feeling soured his taste for tea. Just then the door slid back and out walked Inspector Regulator Daniel Tom.

"Oh, almost didn't see you there." Daniel held a cup of steaming liquid out from his body to avoid being scalded.

Briscoe leapt out of the possible spill zone.

"IR Baker! Didn't think we'd see you so soon after, well, you know."

Briscoe took in Daniel's nervous grin and body language as he hunched as if withdrawing. He didn't know Daniel well, so news of his injury must have already made the rounds.

"Yes, thanks. Rumors of my demise are greatly exaggerated."

Daniel snorted. "IR Granger said as much yesterday."

"Yesterday?" Briscoe leaned in. Now, Daniel had his attention. Instant fear poured through him like cold water dousing his soul since he couldn't get in touch with Fawn most of the day.

Daniel sipped what smelled like coffee. "Yeah. She joined us on a violator retrieval. We nabbed Damoni Brees. Neese thought the violator had info about your death violation."

"Is she alright?"

"Oh yeah. They tried to ambush us, but we took them down."

"Not the violator, Fawn!" Briscoe grabbed Daniel's shoulder.

The java sloshed onto his hand, making Daniel hiss. He snatched himself free and glared at Briscoe.

After switching hands, he said, "She's fine. I guess the medics treated her."

Briscoe inclined his head. "*Merci*."

"No problem." Daniel hurried down the hallway.

The medics? The Fathers!

A thousand scenarios raced through his head.

"BB?"

Briscoe turned to Fawn's call. She'd walked up to him without him realizing it because he was so deep in thought.

He scooped her into a bear hug.

She squirmed. "Stop!"

Laughing, she wiggled out of his embrace. She pulled down her blouse and adjusted her clothes. "You can re-injure yourself. What's gotten into you?"

He did as she asked. His wounds burned but he ignored them. When Daniel had said Fawn needed a medic, his heart pinched in worry. Now that he'd touched her, heard her, and could feel her warm hand, he relaxed. She looked uninjured.

"What are you doing here? What's all this about?" Fawn fluffed her pink collar and checked her black belt. The matching slacks made her seem taller.

"I just heard about the violator retrieval you went on yesterday. Daniel said you needed a medic…"

"Yes, but…"

"I haven't heard from you. You didn't reply to my messages." Briscoe sniffed at her in mock sorrow.

"I left you here," Fawn said.

"Nah. You left me to be driven mad by an annoying n-bot."

Briscoe pulled her into another brief hug. "You smell good."

"Of course, I do. I showered."

"Why are you here?" Fawn asked again as they both headed back to their office.

Once inside, Briscoe eased into his chair. "I'm told you, the n-bot's super annoying, but quit stalling. What are the leads?"

Fawn leaned against her desk. "First, be honest…"

"I'm always honest."

"…how angry is Raul at me?"

"On a scale of one to ten?" Briscoe quirked an eyebrow.

"Yeah."

"100."

"Wow." Fawn winced.

"Give him time. He had a quite a scare. You know the carnage he sees coming into the ER every day. My incident triggered all those fears."

"Mine too."

Briscoe sighed. "Now, tell me about the viable leads you found after I bowed out."

Fawn turned around to her desk. "Well, I'm still waiting for Mario from robotics to get back to me, but considering how much was in that workshop, we may be waiting awhile. I did learn from the hacker we picked up yesterday that Leonard Cho had a full-blown robot addiction."

Briscoe gaped. "Well! Could explain why his

bedroom had such a funk. Did vio give us any results on the sheets?"

"Nothing yet. They're always backed up." Fawn sat down and swept left on the smart glass to wake the computer up. "But, the hacker, Damoni, told me Cho had been suspended from AGEH on more than one occasion. We need to talk to Dr. Baldwin again."

"She's a person of interest, but how credible is Damoni? She's a hacker. Is this true intel or some rank rumor at the job site?" Briscoe drummed his fingers on the desk.

"I found her pretty credible. It gives us an opportunity to question Dr. Baldwin about the working relationship Cho had. If his whole life was his work, then we have to dig into his work life more."

"True. Are you all right? Daniel said you needed a medic?"

Fawn shrugged. "I'm fine. Regulator Ado didn't fare as well. It happened so fast. They escalated so quickly."

Briscoe pursed his lips as if he had a bad taste in his mouth. "Anything Neese does escalates into a situation. What possessed you to go along with him?"

Fawn sighed. "I dunno. Neese was so fixated on stopping those hackers, he was careless. I wanted the lead on Cho's death. I mean, I don't want to leave it with you after…"

"...Friday. Tell me everything." Briscoe straightened in his chair. "From the beginning, please."

As Fawn spoke, Briscoe's ears burned in anger. Neese had acted cold and calloused, not considering the lives of both the violators and regulators. He'd behaved as if he had nothing to lose, when in fact he did. The line between ambition and apathy could be thin.

Fawn's voice changed and it brought his attention fully back to her.

"What's the medic's name again?" Briscoe suppressed the smile tugging on his lips.

"Torey."

"Oh, you like her," Briscoe teased. He could hear it in her voice; the hint of joy, a droplet of attraction.

Fawn waved him off. "She's a bright person with an infectious smile. She probably was being kind—the training, you know. That's how medics are."

"Is that what you want it to be? It sounds like sparks ignited between you two. You sound like she lit your match. I mean…"

"Stop with the fire analogies."

"Well, you sure stamped that out."

"BB!"

"Okay, okay, but you were glowing when you talked about her just now. Plus, you're gonna miss my calculating mind when you're gone."

Fawn's grin dissolved. "I am, and I do like her, but I'm leaving in three days. What's the point?"

"I ask again. It is something you want?"

"Moving." Fawn held up three fingers.

"That's not an answer."

"I know."

Briscoe didn't push it any further. He rubbed his bandaged belly lightly, an agony lingered there, but he didn't want to worry Fawn.

It did please him to see her taking an interest in someone. Bruce had been damn near five years ago.

"You okay?" His eagle-eyed partner looked across her desk at him.

"Aren't we a pair?"

Fawn chuckled. "Fuck, yeah."

The Anderson Clinic hadn't changed since their visit the day before. However, although the building hadn't changed, the way Fawn and Briscoe were treated had. As soon as they entered the clinic's doors, the receptionist waved them forward.

"Inspectors!" he called, leaning out the window. He wore a similar gray uniform to the nurses, and his face bore floral facial tattoos. "Go on through!"

Fawn nodded, but her belly tingled. Security bots waited with hushed mechanical humming as she and Briscoe passed through yet another set of doors into the patient waiting area. Their blowing warmth contrasted with their cold, painted faces.

"Follow, please."

Briscoe scoffed. "Adding please to an order doesn't mean it isn't an order."

They walked, flanked by the bots, down a long corridor. The environment hadn't changed since yesterday, either. Quiet conversations snaked out to greet them as they passed. The blackened windows of Cho's workstation prevented them from spying anything. That *was* new.

"Looks like their cover up is underway," Fawn whispered to Briscoe.

"Uh huh."

Their miniature entourage halted at the door to a corner office with floor to ceiling windows looking out over the ecosystem. Dr. Baldwin's name was emblazoned on the door. The woman herself met them as the door opened.

As before, she wore a white lab coat, blue button-down shirt and dark slacks. Her hair had been cinched at the neck and small diamond earrings adorned her ears.

"Inspectors. Your connect said you had an urgent update."

"Yes," Fawn said. "Is there some place we can speak?"

"Right. Come in." Dr. Baldwin stepped back into her office and gestured for them to enter.

As they sat down on a loveseat, Briscoe said, "Tell us from the outset of the investigation when you have information. We'll determine what's pertinent."

"What do you mean?" Dr. Baldwin sat behind her desk, a thin smart-glass topped rectangular piece of furniture. She gave them a flash of teeth.

In most interviews, an inspector built rapport to put the person at ease.

Not Briscoe.

He confronted her.

"You omitted some alarming information about Dr. Cho," Fawn said.

"I'm not clear on what you mean." Dr. Baldwin was no longer smiling.

Briscoe fed her a little bit of information. "We were transporting a hacker to headquarters and she provided some intel about Dr. Cho."

Dr. Baldwin blinked. "Is this supposed to mean something to me?"

Fawn and Briscoe exchanged looks. *How many secrets was she hiding from them?*

"We learned of Dr. Cho's affection for bots and how he'd been suspended on several occasions. Please tell us more," Fawn said.

Dr. Baldwin sighed. She glanced around her office as if seeking protection or some place to hide. With manicured fingers, she swept her hand across the smart glass and called up the computer access embedded in the surface. She entered a password and her fingerprint. The windows turned opaque, closing it off from passing eavesdroppers.

"I see. I tried to give us some privacy. Now, everyone has the unsavory secrets." Dr. Baldwin pursed her lips.

"Was this an employee coming undone?" Briscoe asked. "We've been to his apartment."

Dr. Baldwin paled beneath her delicate makeup.

"We saw the closet." Fawn didn't want to give the secret room away, if Baldwin didn't know about it, but the hint hit home.

"I see." Dr. Baldwin cleared her throat. "Lately, Leonard—uh, Dr. Cho—seemed a bit out of it."

"What did you expect? You hired a robot addict in a robotics area," Briscoe said. "The man must've been constantly tempted and failing quite as often."

"Truthfully, inspector? I expected an affair, infidelity."

Tears rimmed the green eyes behind Dr. Baldwin's glasses.

Tears? Why is she suddenly so emotional?

Fawn sighed. She knew it. Baldwin *had been* holding back, but she hadn't expected *this*.

Briscoe gave an audible gasp. "More than colleagues then." Briscoe made it a statement.

"Yes, I apologize for not telling you yesterday, but well, Dr. Cho's personal issues weren't mine to share."

"He's dead." Briscoe spread his arms as if to say, 'let's get on with it.'

"It was instantaneous for me. The moment I met him. He was a beautiful man. Smart. Warm. Leonard had an interesting personality. I knew I wanted him."

"Was it mutual?" Fawn asked.

"Eventually."

"Go on," Fawn said.

"Leonard—uh, Dr. Cho—was curious and brilliant. He and I were friends. We had some good times."

"They're all good times when you remember them." Fawn took out her tablet to take notes.

"It's hardly good knowing you were some man's good time." This last came out as a croak.

Dr. Baldwin took in a deep breath. Her cold nature thawed. With watery eyes, she looked down at her hands, folded in her lap. "The last time we talked, I lost my temper with him. I suspected him of having an affair with someone he worked with."

"Was it true?"

"No, none of it."

"Did he react emotionally? Physically?" Briscoe raised his eyebrows, but he switched up tactics.

Dr. Baldwin crossed her arms. "It infuriated him."

"Tell me about the suspicions." Fawn didn't want Dr. Baldwin to get mired in the personal relationship with Cho. She had motive to kill him, but Fawn wanted the details Damoni had given her.

"Well, about about six months into his tenure here, he started to do out of character things. To be transparent, I didn't want him back after my suspicions were aroused."

"Why not?"

Her shoulders slouched. "He'd changed overnight. The fantasy absorbed him. His paranoia spiraled into this 'us versus others' faux reality."

"That's not the only reason why he was suspended. Was it?" Fawn could tell, Dr. Baldwin hadn't given them everything.

"This has to be off the record. I will deny everything if you reveal any of what I'm about to tell you." Dr. Baldwin tapped an icon on her desk.

Fawn's tablet winked out, shutting down immediately.

One look from Briscoe told her the same had happened to him. If they had any connectivity to The District's net, it was gone. No secret stealth recordings.

"We're trying to keep this from dissolving into chaos."

"I'm glad we understand each other. Now, about six months ago, Leonard became delusional. He demanded to develop more human characteristics in the nurse bots —to give them more compassion. The board rejected his proposal. It was a crushing blow to Leonard's ego. He lost it. Threatened the board members with death. As a result, he was suspended."

"No one reported the threats?" Briscoe slipped his tablet back into his coat's interior pocket.

Dr. Baldwin shook her head. "I'm surprised *you* even know about this personnel issue."

"The AGEH isn't in the business of airing their soiled laundry," Fawn said.

Dr. Baldwin smiled.

"Did any of his colleagues display a grievance toward him?" Fawn asked.

"Yes, but I cannot give you their names without going through legal," Dr. Baldwin said.

"Why not? We're off the record," Briscoe said.

"Are we?" Dr. Baldwin said, her grin tightening.

"We're sorry for your loss. Help us find out what happened," Briscoe said.

Dr. Baldwin sniffed, but no more tears fell. "I don't know what happened to Dr. Cho."

"Did you go out to lunch with him? See anything suspicious?" Briscoe stood up.

Dr. Baldwin snorted, then caught herself. "Not hardly. AGEH demands fast turnaround. I drank a protein shake. Security can provide you the cafeteria footage."

"Dr. Cho had only one thing—AGEH. You had a relationship with him that transcended the lab. Surely there's more here," Fawn pushed. "His whole life was this company."

Dr. Baldwin gripped her chair's arm tight, her

knuckles white against its gray surface. "Look, I don't know who killed him. I have no idea. Now I have a busy day. Please contact our attorney if there is anything more you need for your investigation."

Briscoe nodded. "Thank you for your time."

Fawn could make out the grief in the other woman's eyes. Dr. Baldwin had loved Dr. Cho. She didn't kill him.

"You're welcome." Dr. Baldwin keyed in the passcode and the windows cleared. "No matter what happened between us, there was still love."

They shook hands in farewell. Dr. Baldwin gave them a weak smile.

Fawn held onto her hand. "One more question."

"Yes?" Dr. Baldwin's face tightened.

"What's your personal expertise?"

"Genetics. I work on hatchlings." Dr. Baldwin yanked her hand free and retreated behind the safety of her glass door.

Outside the entrance to her office, the security bots greeted Fawn and Briscoe.

"Follow, please."

Fawn wasn't sure they'd ever left.

Once they were seated in Briscoe's wauto once more, he scratched behind his ear. "We need evidence to implicate her. Motive of 'scorned partner' isn't enough. We need a whole lot more."

"People have been convicted of violations for less."

"True, but we need to dig deeper, like to Atlantis."

"Atlantis is in the ocean. You can't dig to it."

"Exactly my point."

"She's desperate. Why?"

"Pressed, I'd say—but she's in a hell of a position." Briscoe took out a cigarette and lit it. "People are secretive around regs anyway, especially AGEH."

Fawn's resolve became stronger. "Do you think they reconciled their differences?"

"Dunno. She's definitely driven and determined. I want to see if audio/visuals had any luck pulling any footage from the craft and then the on-the-ground eyes," Briscoe said.

"We're waiting on a lot of potential leads."

"We should eat."

At the mention of food, her stomach rumbled in agreement. She'd only had coffee—now around the lunch hour, she realized her hunger.

"Yes. Let's get some fuel. Where you wanna go?" Fawn said.

Briscoe blew several rings before answering. "Any place that has syth tea."

CHAPTER TWELVE

AFTER LUNCH, Fawn and Briscoe returned to their office. Garlic lingered on her clothing, but the wheat pasta with mushrooms and garlic sauce at Big Mike's never disappointed. Full and satisfied, she plopped down in her chair and woke up her desk computer.

She called up the violation scene images to review them again. They needed a clue, something to push them in the right direction.

"Reviewing the case file may put us closer to the killer," she said to Briscoe who sat at his desk sipping tea.

Something tugged in Fawn's memory. "Are these all the violation scene jpegs in this file?"

"Yes." Briscoe nodded.

Fawn touched the glass and scrolled through the images until she found one of Dr. Cho's body and the debris around him. With the press of the magnifying glass, she enlarged the image to find an object slightly obscured behind the victim.

"There!" Fawn drew a box around the image with her index finger and highlighted it. "You see it?"

"It's a robot." Briscoe got up and came over to her desk. He leaned in closer.

"An n-bot. Damaged." Fawn pointed to the dented section of the robot's lower region.

The robot didn't look just damaged but assaulted. Scratches raked across its metallic body. Dents and small circular indentations dotted the area around the viewing section.

Fawn looked back to the photos. "Where is this bot now?"

"In evidence. We'll have to get it called up to robotics." Briscoe returned to his desk and began typing on the surface.

"I want to see it."

"Okay. But do we really need to see the robot?" Briscoe finished typing and crossed his arms. "It may not be related."

Fawn *tsk*ed at him. "BB, Dr. Cho worked exclusively with n-bots. There was n-bot oil in his wounds. Let's take a look at the bot found near him."

"Covering all our bases." Briscoe reached into his pocket and took out his cigarette case.

"Right." Fawn pointed at his case. "The coincidences are piling up."

"I'm waiting on Mario to tell us to come up. In the meantime, I'm going to smoke."

Briscoe got up, grabbed his coat, and left. He

could've smoked at this desk with a foghog, but sometimes he liked being outside the office. Parts of him probably missed being a uniformed regulator out on patrol. The desk sometimes made him feel trapped.

Fawn stood up too. *A mid-afternoon coffee will give me a little jolt.*

She exited her office and was headed to the break-room when Torey walked by, stopped, and shot Fawn a soft smile.

Fawn froze mid-stride.

Torey came toward her, her shoulder-length braids bouncing as she walked. She wore her medic uniform, navy boots, and a thin gold chain around her neck. Her sleeves had been pushed up and the light reflected off her silver-toned watch.

Briscoe's words came roaring back, echoing in Fawn's ears, faint encouragement.

Could this beautiful woman be interested—in me?

Fawn allowed herself this small foray into the possible before mentally slamming the door shut.

"Hi, Inspector," Torey said, once she reached Fawn.

Fawn managed a small wave of greeting. "Um, call me Fawn."

Torey rubbed her arm. "Fawn. That's a nice, soft name."

Inside, Fawn shook like a lonely leaf in a tornado. "Thanks...I think."

She fought to keep her tone steady, but she vibrated inside.

Torey laughed, but then both of them cast nervous

glances at each other. Every time she met Torey's deep, hazel eyes, a wild tingling fluttered through her.

"So, um, what brings you to headquarters?" Fawn put her hands in the pockets of her pants to stop fidgeting.

"I was giving a statement to IR Tom," Torey said. "I did hope I'd see you."

"Oh?"

"Yeah," Torey said with a grin, "I wanted to ask you to dinner or a coffee the other night, but it looked like you'd had one hell of a day."

"Yeah…" Fawn's ears burned.

"You almost got deleted."

"Yeah, true. Oh, um," Fawn stammered and struggled to find words. It was like someone had deleted her ability to formulate ideas and communicate them. Her heavy tongue wouldn't move. "Well, thank you for the invitation. Dinner sounds nice."

"I hear a but…" Torey's smile dimmed.

"I'm relocating at the end of the week." Fawn groaned inside, but she had to tell the truth. Going on a date when she'd be thousands of miles away in three days didn't sit well with her.

Torey's face brightened. "Ah, so we can make it a going away celebration dinner. How about tonight? Tomorrow you're probably packing and getting all the last minute stuff done. Right?"

Fawn's world kind of stopped right there for a few moments.

She still wants to go out with me.

"Yes, I'd like that, but I'm working an active death violation. Things get pretty unpredictable."

"Same here! We both thrive on helping others. So if nothing else, let's grab a coffee in the morning if tonight gets away from us. How's that?"

"Deal."

They exchanged connects and as she leaned in for a quick hug, Fawn smelled lavender. Torey's scent made her smile. It was a lot like Torey, soft, but tough.

"We'll touch base later." Torey slid her handheld into her uniform's interior pocket.

"I'd like that. Yes," Fawn said.

They stood there, trapped in the budding glow of attraction. Neither wanted to break the spell by stepping away first, for fear of losing its warmth. There was only Torey in Fawn's consciousness, so when Briscoe touched her shoulder and called her name, she jumped.

"Ah!" Fawn grabbed her heart.

"I did call your name." Briscoe spoke to Fawn, but his gaze was on Torey. "You are?"

"Torey Graham." She inclined her head at Briscoe as if to say it was his turn.

"Inspector Regulator Briscoe Baker, her partner."

"I'll be on my way, Fawn," Torey said, and then, turning to Briscoe, "Nice to meet you."

"Likewise," Briscoe said.

Once Torey disappeared down the central stairway, Briscoe leaned into Fawn. "She *is* pretty."

"Don't start." Fawn resumed her trek to the break-room.

Briscoe followed behind her. “I haven’t even begun! Tell me the details. What’s she doing up here?”

Other inspectors hung out in the rectangular space. Some were seated on barstools that lined a narrow counter running the length of the back wall. Others sat at bistro-style tables, only big enough for two, but—as often was habit— clusters of three or more pulled up their chairs around the little tables anyway.

Fawn went to the coffee maker, picked up a ceramic mug, and stuck it under the spout. She punched in her selection and within seconds it poured out in steaming fury.

“There’s nothing to tell.” Fawn rolled her eyes. “We have a case to solve. Let’s focus on it. Did Mario notify us yet?”

“I dunno. I haven’t been back to the office. After surviving the stairs, I saw you with her. So, I came over.”

“Okay, let’s see if he’s replied. It’s been long enough. We sure he’s in today?”

“Yeah. He’s marked ‘available’.” Briscoe scrolled through his handheld before looking back up at her.

They left the break-room in silence.

Once back at his desk, Briscoe swept left and scanned his notifications. “Yeah, Mario said he’s ready.”

Fawn didn’t bother sitting at her desk. Briscoe shrugged out of his coat, hung it up and together they headed up to AV & Media’s third floor offices.

The Audio/Visual and Media section consumed more than three-quarters of the entire third floor of Regulator Headquarters. Each of the large, allocated spaces had been divided into departments. Fawn and Briscoe walked by the Audio, Digital Video, Internet, and Crypto departments, and then finally came to Robotics.

They walked into the noisy space. Mario waved them over to his workstation. The wide-open floor plan resembled a wauto repair shop—but for robots. Bot parts littered every inch of available surface, on tables, on shelves, in boxes, and in various states of repair or dismantling. Along the walls, computers flickered in an array of different lights and wires shot out like tentacles from the boards, a thousand skinny black limbs, reaching for the right connection.

Mario wore his gray regulator uniform and protective googles. "Hey, sorry about the wait. Today's been mad."

He held a tablet in one hand. "You wanted to look at the n-bot from the death violation scene down on F Street."

"Yeah." Fawn nodded.

"I had to get it called up from evidence," Mario explained. On the tele-monitor behind him, he loaded the nurse bot's schematics. "Should be here any minute. I put in the request about 20 minutes ago."

Sure enough, one of the vioTechs brought it in on a floating trolley. The tech transferred it onto the metallic table beside Mario's workstation.

"I'm transferring ownership to you." The white clad vioTech held out a handheld.

Mario verified his identity with his thumbprint. She left without a glance at Fawn or Briscoe.

Briscoe clucked his tongue. "She's nice."

"Focus, BB" Fawn gestured to the robot.

Mario smirked, but he didn't comment. He checked

the bot on his table to verify where it had come from. The three of them crowded around the egg-shaped machine. Mario reviewed his tablet's screen. He rolled the egg-shaped robot onto its back and secured it with rubber straps to the table. The robot bore deep scratches, gouges, paint transfer, and dents in the front of its body. The two bent, mechanical arms remained stuck at awkward angles.

"Two robotic hands attached to two arm joints have been damaged. The right hand shows signs of direct impact from a blunt instrument."Mario held it out for them to see. "It won't be in service anymore. The repairs required would cost more than the machine itself."

"For the arm?" Briscoe raised an eyebrow in surprise.

"No, for the entire bot. It's been severely damaged and modified." Mario gestured to the gouges and the other scratches along the robot's finish.

"Dr. Cho's umbrella had traces of the same oil found on his hands and in his wounds. Trace found paint from the umbrella's handle here on the bot." Fawn read aloud from the trace report on her tablet, pointing to a spot on the n-bot. "Trace report just came in."

Briscoe looked up at Fawn. "He would have traces, wouldn't he? Cho works with the stuff at his job. He gets oil on his hands, he touches his umbrella, and then it gets everywhere."

Mario said, "We did find oil on his clothing at the apartment as well as in the workstation, but the composite is strange. We are doing further tests on it—well, Trace is. It isn't uniform. Also, vioTechs discovered puncture wounds in Cho's sheets and mattress. I won't speculate about why. I'll leave that up to you, but I think I know *how*."

Mario removed the robot's front panel.

Fawn said, "Whoa. I'm sure the AGEH doesn't know about *this*."

"The more we delve into the investigation, the stranger it gets." Fawn shook her head.

"That *is* unnerving," Briscoe said, nodding at the n-bot.

The robot's front compartment contained a third, smaller mechanical arm, but instead of a hand, it ended with a laser-gun. It appeared to be dislodged and it jutted out of the compartment usually reserved for medical supplies.

No one had ditched the gun at the scene.

The n-bot took it with them.

"Ironic, isn't it? Here's a weapon in the place where the healing items should go." Fawn reached out to touch the laser-gun, but Mario caught her hand.

"Don't. I'm sure this killed a man." He guided her hand away. "Let me dismantle it first. I wanna make sure it's offline with no hidden protocols, like the one you found, IR Baker."

Fawn moved a safe distance away.

"Never take an umbrella to a gun fight." Briscoe shook his head. "Damn shame."

Mario cleared his throat, but Fawn couldn't tell if the engineer laughed or not.

"I bet it will match the signature of the blast on the body." Briscoe stuck a cigarette into his mouth and quirked an eyebrow when Mario wagged his finger in warning.

"No smoking in here, friend. All these chemicals and gases..."

Briscoe growled, but put it away. He paced between the smart-glass boards and the shelves of robot parts.

Mario pointed at the small compartment. "It's a similar modification to the one we found earlier, except instead of a knife, this one has a laser-gun. The security bot attacked IR Baker, and this appears to be an extension of the same programming, but I'd have to run the code and dig deeper to be sure. We found scores of plans, schematics, and proposals for further development of the nurse bots, including some language that seemed to focus on cybernetics in the hidden workshop."

Fawn's eyebrows shot into her hair. "What?"

Mario lowered his voice. "We found documentation pointing to modification of nurse bots to become lethal, smaller security options for home protection. AGEH had mock marketing pamphlets drawn up. Dr. Cho had them in his workstation's computer. He'd stored them in the cloud, but we were able to break his code and review them. His hubris got the better of him. He thought no one would find his secret lab, because he barely had any security on any of the files there." Mario shook his head.

"What are you saying, Mario? In plain language." Briscoe leaned in close, over the n-bot.

"He's saying this nurse bot killed Dr. Cho," Fawn said.

Briscoe gaped at them. "I'm sorry. It sounds like we're grasping at straws here."

"We've narrowed it down to two options. Either the bot killed him, or the bot killed him." Fawn pointed at the laser-gun nestled in the smaller compartment.

Briscoe shook his head.

"I can't hear you. My mind went blank after you said killer robot."

CHAPTER THIRTEEN

"WE'RE WORKING ON A THEORY, IR Baker." Mario connected some wires to the nurse bot and the computer. Now, tethered together, his tablet lit up.

Briscoe was frantic, but for the moment, he agreed, "Fine, but it's a crazy theory."

"What theory doesn't begin as something labeled crazy?" Mario cajoled.

"I wonder why it killed him?" Fawn stared at the defective robot. "Why would Dr. Cho give it a gun? I mean, it would have to be him that altered the bot to carry this. Right?"

"I suspect so," Mario said.

Briscoe shrugged. "It rules out all the usual emotional suspects. Robots don't feel envy, love, greed, or anger. Those are human inventions."

"Can you analyze the programming?" Fawn asked Mario. "I want to know what its last series of commands were."

Mario looked up at her from the robot. "Yes. As I said, I am already working on it, but it's a lot so I'm also working with a programmer."

"Would it be in the code? No doubt the killer erased all traces of himself." Briscoe added, "I would if I wanted to program a robot to kill him."

"If it was a premeditated homicide, maybe," Fawn said. "The violence on the body is chaotic, disorganized. Not clean or clinical like a robot would normally do. Malfunction maybe?"

Briscoe folded his arms low on his chest and chewed on his cigarette. "Robots—especially n-bots—don't just go berserk and kill. They're checked for safety by the District Robotics Safety Association. There are thousands of these in operation."

"If they malfunction, they can," Mario said. "You don't read the e-files."

"I want to see what happened. We need the CCTV footage." Fawn scanned her tablet. "It's still not available. *Grrrr*."

Mario chuckled behind her. "Sometimes if you go see them in person, they'll call up the vids for you to scan yourself."

"Seriously?" Fawn met Briscoe's amused expression.

"Yeah, if you want to scan through hours of footage, they'll let you." Mario shrugged.

"Come on then, BB." Fawn started for the door. "Oh, Mario, let us know what you find."

"It might be a while, there's tons of code to go through," Mario glanced at the screen where scores of rolling string commands filled the monitor.

"Okay. Thank you."

They left Robotics and walked down the long corridor to Vids.

"I freaked out." Briscoe tucked his cigarette back into its sleek hard-case.

"Couldn't tell." Fawn peered over at him.

He elbowed her.

"I'm serious! I own one of those."

Fawn patted her shoulder. "I know, but I don't think this is a mass robotic issue. Your n-bot doesn't have a weapon in its storage compartment. Raul would've known. He's the one who restocks it. Right?"

"Right," Briscoe said.

Inside the Vids workspace, rows of hackers sat at circular consoles with illuminated keyboards and earbuds within a dark room. A hush filled the room. Screens flickered. Others showed rolling videos. She couldn't name a single one of them, except Regulator Kim, who served as department manager.

"Inspector Regulator Granger—oh, and I see Inspector Regulator Baker. How can I help you?" Regulator Kim sat at the main desk. She directed the traffic and managed the AV Department. Her purple afro glowed in the shadowy room. Her one-piece regulator uniform revealed her quite-pregnant frame.

"Always so formal, Kim." Briscoe reached out to hug her.

She rose from her chair and gave him a one-armed hug. "There's much more of me now, IR Baker."

Fawn smiled. "Congratulations!"

Kim rubbed her bulging belly. "Thanks. Tyshawn and I are quite excited."

"As you should be!" Briscoe gushed.

"Enough about me and little one here, what can I do for you?" Kim eased back into her seat.

"We would like to see the footage for death violation, S12-052203-A1." Fawn extended her arm, so Kim could scan her wrist for verification.

"All right. I'll have it queued up in viewing room one." Kim waved goodbye as Fawn and Briscoe headed through the shadowy dark.

"I hate watching vids," Briscoe whispered.

"I know," Fawn whispered back.

She didn't love it either. It took concentration and sharp eyes. Even with those qualities, she'd end up scanning the same footage over and over again, hoping for something to pop out from the previous viewing. It was literally watching the same scene on repeat until one's eyes bled.

Or she discovered a clue.

The quality of the vids varied from location to location throughout The District. Wealthier sectors could afford better cameras and poorer sections tended to have large parts of their sections with black outs—where no cameras existed.

They entered the tight, square room. On the opposite side of the space, across from the entrance, hung a smartglass board. Two tiny folding chairs rested in front of the board. Fawn sat down first, and then Briscoe took the second seat. Once seated, the video data the vioTechs had collected launched.

In front of them, a remote control allowed them to *rewind, pause, play* and *fast forward*. In the lower right, a time and date stamp appeared on the footage. They waited as the replay of Dr. Cho's trip from the cargo craft stop began.

Soon, a male subject entered the area. He fit Dr. Cho's description. The clothing matched what they now had in evidence. The day unfolded for him. Fawn watched for anything the vioTechs had missed. If they'd even gotten around to viewing this video yet.

On the first run through, nothing unusual stood out to her.

"There goes your promising lead," Briscoe said, crossing his legs.

She understood Briscoe's disillusionment and doubt. She didn't trust service bots as a rule, so she didn't own any. Most places used them in their businesses and homes. They'd become a ubiquitous part of The District's life.

The idea of one going off programming and killing someone shook her to her core. It was literally many people's worse nightmare. Consumers' sense of safety would be shattered if this got out. No way this information could get out to the public.

But they had a duty to follow the evidence no matter how unsettling the path.

"BB, you know one viewing is never enough to see everything. Play it again."

"Starting at time elapsed 15:03." Briscoe huffed, but pressed PLAY. "Fawn, if we can't trust our robotic engineers…"

"We can. I believe we can trust the engineers to want to keep this little mess quiet. Robotics is a huge business. No one wants this getting out there."

"You heard Mario. It's been approved already. Pamphlets and stuff." Briscoe kept his voice low, barely audible over the video's rain shower, honking traffic, and section noise.

"Look, BB—Cho is headed in the direction of the Anderson Clinic. Look what is about six steps behind him."

Briscoe's eyes widened. "I'll be damned."

An n-bot hovered behind Dr. Cho's lanky stride and bright blue umbrella. In the sidewalk congestion, the bot blended in, just like any other service robot. Its gray exterior blurred with the dreary day.

Fawn shook her head. "He must've tried to defend himself as the n-bot started to attack."

"The video expands that far but the other camera that picks up that section was down for updates. It's a blind spot." Briscoe commented and pointed at the blip as the camera switched feeds to show Cho's body sprawled in the street.

"So many people saw him, and they refused to intervene. They went on about their lives, to their destinations, and priorities. No one cared about this man's life." Fawn sighed. "They didn't even bother to record it with their handhelds."

Briscoe said, "The net is saturated with violence. This isn't anything new."

"A robot killing a human being?" Fawn turned to look fully at him. "You really *don't* read the e-news files.

They're filled with robot malfunction stories and maimed or accidentally killed people. Those don't even make it to the fourth page. Those reports are buried in the back with UFO sightings and sexy bot services."

No more fruitless efforts to identify Dr. Cho's violator.

Here it was—evidence.

She just didn't like it.

"All classified files for n-bots. Dr. Cho would eventually succumb to his injuries according to Dr. Rycroft's report. The defensive wounds and the umbrella proved he fought for his life." Fawn swallowed the lump in her throat.

"And lost," Briscoe added.

By the time they returned to their office, Briscoe only wanted two things—tea and cake. Plant-based eggs and honey in Raul's hands became moist, sweet, deliciousness. Paired with apricot syth tea, Briscoe would dissolve into a human ball of gooeyness and joy. As he let Fawn out of the wauto, near her areocycle, his thoughts blotted out the revelation of Dr. Leonard Cho's death violator, with saccharine images of artfully decorated cake.

"BB, are you sure you're alright? You look a little green around the gills." Fawn bent down to talk through the passenger window.

"Nothing a little tea and sweets can't fix." Briscoe forced the tremble out of his voice. He didn't want her to worry, but he had a nurse bot at home.

Like literally everyone in The District.

Except Luddites like Fawn.

"Mario said he'd be running the program all night, so he'll connect with us as soon as it delivers an answer."

Briscoe nodded. He wanted to go home and snuggle Raul.

"He did say, the n-bot's registration belongs to the Anderson Clinic. The programming code signature is the victim's."

"Cho was a robotic expert," Briscoe said. "This only proves the nurse bot was his."

"Right, and ties it back to the AGEH."

"Where he worked," Briscoe said. "This could just be an accidental death."

"There's nothing accidental about a laser-gun blast to the chest." Fawn walked off.

"Hey! Hey! Fawn!" Briscoe called out to her.

She returned and crouched back down to the passenger window.

"Yeah?"

Briscoe sobered. "You're leaving in a few days."

"Yeah."

He looked at her. "Get back in. Let's go grab a coffee and cake—well I hate coffee, but you know what I mean."

Fawn hesitated.

"Then we can go check out Anderson Clinic again," Briscoe added. "Do some surveillance one last time. You in?"

Fawn sighed. "Pull my arm, why don't you?"

He wanted to go home, but the days he had left with Fawn were few. He could count them on one hand.

Fawn opened the door and got back in the wauto.

"Did you have other plans?" Briscoe chuckled. She never had plans.

"Actually, BB, I did."

"Really? No. Wait. Torey?"

Fawn nodded. "She and I can get coffee tomorrow. Let's close this case, partner."

He smiled at her for a long moment, taking in the fact she'd skip out on a date to hang out doing boring regulator stuff with him, and then he started the flight sequence.

In minutes, they flew up into the elevated lanes and The District's velvety night.

The rain had finally stopped, but dark clouds drifted across the night sky. The Anderson Clinic remained closed. Briscoe played a game on his tablet. He'd collapsed the wauto's steering wheel to give him more lap space. He and Fawn sat in the leather seats of his luxury vehicle. It hovered inches above the street.

"No one is there." He glanced up at Fawn, before diving back into his game.

"Someone is there because the rear interior lights are still on."

"The cleaning bots."

"They don't need lights. They have night vision."

Fawn's neck ached and the pain reliever waned.

They'd been seated in Briscoe's wauto for about two hours. When they'd arrived, a mob of people stood around outside, complaining about the clinic's abrupt closing.

"What do you think the AGEH is doing?" Briscoe asked. "None of the people I spoke to seemed to know why the clinic suddenly closed."

Fawn sighed as she leaned back in the seat. "Hiding the evidence—but one person I spoke to said they closed for emergency cleaning of a chemical spill. Desperate conspiracy anyone?"

"By the fathers, they need to get more creative. They've been using chemical spills since Roswell. And you know how old that is? Right?"

"Don't you think it's odd Cho knew robotics, and Baldwin's expertise is genetics?"

"No. I'm good at clothes. You're good at weaponry. People have different expertise."

"What if, BB, the n-bot had a consciousness and got some of those emotions we talked about? What if this was a result of pent-up or misplaced rage?"

Briscoe looked up at her. "Science fiction. Write that up. It'd be a great story."

Fawn punched him. "I'm serious."

"Ow! Besides you know cyborgs are violations. It carries a decade in the cradle."

"In *this* territory, but Cho wasn't from here. He came from the Cali Province. Who knows what's legal and permissible there? It could've been standard practice for him to link the two—machinery and humankind."

Briscoe put down his tablet. Now she had his attention.

"I'm sure the AGEH would find that research suitable. They've already created hatchlings. What if he brought the knowledge with him to do that work?" Fawn said. "There's no sense in asking Dr. Baldwin. I'm not 100% sold on the story she gave us today. She's too loyal to the company."

"No? Didn't believe she and Leonard were partners?"

"Did you? We and vioTech went through that apartment. There were no signs of a female anywhere. The only DNA found was Cho's. The only body fluids were Cho's."

Briscoe shrugged. "Maybe they took the play to her house. I wouldn't take my lover to the bachelor disaster he called home."

Fawn laughed. "I keep telling you, not everyone has an amazing Raul, like you."

"I know. I know." Briscoe grinned. "How's Torey? She isn't mad about tonight?"

Fawn checked her handheld. "No. We're on for coffee at Sweet Mama's in the morning. This isn't serious, BB. She knows I'm moving."

"Ah." Briscoe picked up his tablet again. "I see."

Fawn elbowed him. "Stop it."

"How deep do you think the lies go?" Briscoe wondered aloud. Then he chuckled. "The AGEH would've swept in there to head off the unfolding scandal. I bet if we connected tomorrow, we'd find Dr. Baldwin on extended holiday leave."

"Most likely." Fawn accessed the vioTech trace report on her tablet.

The flow of adrenaline poured through her—the feeling of discovery, of placing her hands on the truth. She stood at the precipice of closing her case. She glanced over at Briscoe.

Our case.

She scrolled through the reports seeking more clues to solidify their working theory.

"Cho's renter's insurance inventory included several n-bots. One of the serial numbers matches the one currently in evidence," Briscoe announced. "And you thought I was playing a game."

"Damn. He did it. His experimented with the bot and it killed him." Fawn rubbed her face. "You believe this, BB? Cho modified that nurse bot to be a weapon."

Briscoe looked outside the window. "The question is, did he do it on his own or with help?"

Fawn sighed. "There's no real way to tell."

"The code," Briscoe said.

"It could've been tampered with by Dr. Baldwin. Sometimes partnerships splinter."

"Maybe Mario will have something for us tomorrow." Briscoe massaged his neck. "We're not getting in there tonight."

"A violent n-bot. Surreal." Fawn stretched. "Why didn't he work on it at the clinic with a staff or at least a team?"

"Clearly because it was a secret. It was in a secret lab," Briscoe said.

"If so, how did it get out, follow Dr. Cho, and kill

him?"

Silence as they both pondered.

"We know intimacy can be an indicator of violence. The Anderson Clinic sent over footage of Dr. Baldwin during the time of the violation, drinking a shake in the cafeteria." Briscoe shut off his tablet. "Based on our estimated timeline, she couldn't have done it."

"Plus, we didn't see her on the vids," Fawn acknowledged, following his train of thought. "That doesn't mean she couldn't have sicced the bot on him."

A chill skated down Fawn's spine at the realization.

"True. Could she have programmed it to kill Cho?" Briscoe put the steering wheel in place and started the flight sequence. "She's a geneticist. I can't see her risking the involvement of another person to help her. Too risky. Hatchlings are still their moneymaker."

"Until five seconds ago, you didn't think she was capable."

"Oh, I believe everyone's capable," Briscoe retorted.

"Word travels fast on the street, but when it comes to jealousy, there's always a breaking point." Fawn crossed her arms.

"Who's she jealous of? She's his boss." Briscoe turned on his lights.

"His bots."

"You're serious?"

"How many people have abandoned their partners for bots?" Fawn looked at Briscoe.

"Ah, yeah. Murphy over in robbery left his partner just two months ago…"

"The best lies, BB, contain a kernel of truth."

CHAPTER FOURTEEN

BY THE TIME Fawn made it back to headquarters, every inch of her ached, but she couldn't get Torey's warm smile out of her head nor the cold realization of Cho's violator.

A bit nauseous and hungry, Fawn didn't bother going back to her office. It had been an incredibly long and confusing day. Fawn made a beeline for her aerocycle. She detached her helmet from the cycle and put it on. In moments, she zipped into the sky, careful of the thinning elevated lanes. Most people who commuted for work had made it home by now. As the hour approached 22:00, Fawn soared. Here, above the cluster of people, buildings, and violence, she was liberated. Flying without the confines of a wauto allowed the wind to rush by her, snatching away stress, and anxiety.

Piloting made her focus. Here, she controlled the path, the speed, and the trajectory of her life—literally.

The wind hurried by as she threw back her head and laughed.

Once Fawn arrived home, she dropped everything inside the door. Satchel, boots, pants, and blouse hit the floor with all the disdain and annoyance she could muster.

"Andre, start my shower."

Sebastian meowed and brushed her ankles, offering his sympathy.

"*Merci.*" She bent down and stroked him. "How'd you know today was a shit day?"

She removed her socks, scooped up her clothes, and padded barefoot to her bedroom. She dumped the items into her hamper before sliding into the steaming hot water. The blue decorative recessed-lighting turned the square room into a lush cocoon of warm water and tulip-smelling soap. Fawn closed her eyes, picked up her poof and soap, and scrubbed the day away.

After she rinsed, dried, and oiled her skin, Fawn pulled on her favorite purple robe and sat on the sofa in her living room, surrounded by pillows. The floor-to-ceiling windows revealed the glittering District lights, each glowing against the unbroken night. Soft music cuddled her, and wine warmed her. Boxes cluttered her space. Sebastian took delighted in exploring them.

"You're right, Seb. This is a great view."

Sebastian leapt onto the sofa. He meowed as if he understood. His glowing, round eyes searched her face.

"What do you think I should do?"

He lay on her feet as if to say, "It has to be your decision."

With her free hand, she stroked his soft fur. He purred in pleasure.

What awaited her in the Southwest? Violations existed in every territory. The job would be similar to that she found here. There'd be no Briscoe. Sure, she'd get a partner, but would she get one like him? One who would understand her condition?

No, there's only one BB.

She'd wrestled with these questions for ages. The ranch felt good—a true escape—but what she ran from would remain. After all, she couldn't escape herself.

The tele-monitor broke through her musings.

"Incoming connect from Torey Lee."

"Answer, audio only." Fawn pulled her robe closer around her body. Her dreadlocks were free, and she'd showered.

A smile flitted across her lips. "'Ello."

Torey's voice poured into Fawn's living room surround speakers.

"*Hola*!" How goes the packing?"

"Slowly. I was just taking a break. What're you up to tonight?"

"Just got off shift. Thought I'd connect. You were on my mind."

"You worked?"

"Yeah. I got called in."

"Good thoughts? Yeah?"

"For sure." Torey's throaty purr at the sentence's end gave Fawn goosebumps.

At a loss for words, Fawn cuddled a sleepy Sebastian. She couldn't fathom the medic wanting to talk to her. It's been a long time since she did this.

"I'm listening," Fawn said.

"Yeah, me too." Torey laughed. "So, um, how was work?" she asked.

"The death violation? It's slow, like my packing."

Torey chuckled. "Are we still on for coffee tomorrow?"

"Yeah. I'm, uh, looking forward to it."

"Me too."

The awkward silence grew, filling the distance between them. Fawn wanted to talk, but what would she say? So many ideas rushed her at once, none of them made it through her lips.

Focus!

"Um, how was *your* work day?"

Torey sighed. "It was a typical night, long. No one died, and that's always the plus. So, a success, I guess. Now I'm going to grab some beef pho, shower, and crash."

"That sounds like heaven. Enjoy your evening." Fawn's grin widened. She meant those words, but the emotion in them embarrassed her. They'd come out on their own.

"You too. See you tomorrow. *Ciao*."

"Yes. Good night."

CHAPTER FIFTEEN

ON A CRISP, fall morning, Fawn sat at one of Sweet Mama's L-shaped, polished wood counters. This one looked out the windowpanes and onto the sidewalk and street. The sweet aroma of vanilla wafted from her date, seated next to her on the neighboring stool.

"This place has the best zero coffee. It tastes so fresh." Torey tapped her mug's lip.

"It does have a rich aroma." Fawn gazed out and over the clear morning sky. Fall in The District seduced people into believing in hope and freedom with its picturesque views and turning leaves.

Fawn turned her attention from the beauty outside to the one seated beside her. Torey's lean frame, poised on the metal barstool, was draped in blue jeans and a black turtleneck. She wore rubber-soled, hunter green boots and silver hoop earrings in descending size. They peeked out from beneath her loose braids.

"You're off today?"

Torey nodded. "How'd you know?"

"I'm an inspector," Fawn said with a small laugh. "Your earrings are a giveaway. Medics don't wear those when working."

Torey titled her head sideways and smiled. "Okay, I like that. We rotate weekends. I'm on tomorrow and Saturday."

"You woke up early just to grab a coffee?" Fawn lowered her mug. "Or are you a morning person?"

Torey chuckled. "Definitely not a morning person, hence the coffee and not breakfast."

"Ah. Yeah. I'm a night owl…"

"Trouble sleeping?"

Fawn hesitated. *How do I answer this question?*

"You're pretty, but those dark circles hint at more than a few restless evenings. You don't have to be an inspector to see that." Torey winked.

Fawn's face warmed. "Job hazard."

"I hear you."

A somewhat comfortable silence descended on them. Each sipped with quick, sidelong glances at the other.

Torey leaned closer to Fawn.

"Thank you for coming to coffee. I'm sure you have so much to do."

"Plenty." Fawn fingered the cup's handle. "This death violation has consumed more time than I thought."

"Work has a way of eroding our time. That's why I have boundaries. Do you have a hobby or something that separates your job from you?" Torey drained the rest of her coffee.

How do I explain that my work life and my home life are

just mirror images of each other without sounding like a workaholic with attachment issues?

Fawn shrugged. "Movies, I guess."

Torey squealed, spooking the neighboring customers. "I love films! Oh. Wait. What genre?"

"Documentaries and cooking shows mostly."

"Ah, romance is my favorite."

Fawn's surprise caught Torey's attention.

"You don't like romances?" Torey rested her hand on her knee and moved back.

"I dunno. They always seem false. By that I mean, the narrative. They uphold old values of love. Real life love brings pain, gouging out one's identity, and leaving ice chunks of loneliness and despair in its wake."

Torey's eyes widened. "I said romance, not horror."

Fawn internally groaned. She'd overshared. Torey's presence made her feel comfortable and calm, but she might have ruined it. When Torey listened to her talk, she made Fawn feel as if only the two of them existed in this section of space and time.

But she'd probably screwed it up.

Torey bit her lower lip and set her mug down on the counter. She placed both hands on her knees and rubbed her thighs. With a slight turn, she faced Fawn.

"I'm sorry that person made you feel like loving you was hard," Torey said.

Fawn's heart pounded at the intensity and sincerity she found in Torey's eyes. The words sunk in. No one had said those to her. They functioned like a thousand keys all unlocking a flood of memories long since locked away in emotional compartments.

Fawn blinked back tears and finished her coffee. "Uh, that went fast. You're right about the flavor."

Torey swallowed. "Oh, yeah. Yeah. This is one of my favorite places."

"It's cozy....and a bit of a throwback." Fawn searched the tiny coffeeshop. Anything to avoid looking at Torey.

Soft music piped in from recessed speakers. The other patrons enjoyed food and drinks at small bistro tables. They consumed media from their tablets and handhelds. Warm colored couches, throw pillows, and decorative rugs outfitted the café. Strange for rugs to be in a place brimming with liquid beverages and crumbly baked goods, but they probably had robots do the cleaning.

Robots.

"Thank you for this, but I have to get back to work." Fawn slid off her stool. She'd taken too much time here already.

"I meant what I said."

Fawn sobered. "Sorry. It caught me off guard."

Torey's hazel eyes narrowed. "It does most people I meet, but in my line of work, I see the fragility of life. You never know when it'll break. It's why I'm blunt, or forward. I tell people how I feel. I don't wait."

"Fragile. That's an interesting way of thinking about life." Fawn put on her coat. "It's certainly fleeting."

"Yeah, fragile. People don't always die. The human body can live through so much, shattering a person into pieces. I can help heal those broken parts, but they're never the same—never whole again. Up here." Torey tapped her temple and then put on her own cranberry coat. It had an A-style cut with the bottom forming a bell shape. It came to mid-thigh. She zipped it without looking at Fawn.

Fawn nodded. "I get it. All I see is the finality of death. We find the person or persons who violated the victim's right to live. Even when we do, it doesn't repair anything."

"No?" Torey flicked her attention to Fawn and then back to the city view as they walked toward the door. "Why do you do it then?"

Fawn paused. *Wouldn't you and my therapist love to know?*

Torey looked back at her. "You don't like it. Is that why you're moving?"

The quick question made Fawn freeze. She was still musing on the previous question and Torey had asked her another.

They exited Sweet Mama's glowing warmth into the early morning workday. In the distance, elevated lanes became less and less clear as commuters clotted up the space. With it came the din of The District awaking.

Torey grinned. "Sorry! I'm all in your personal space."

Fawn offered a weak smile. "It did feel a bit like a job interview."

"Sorry. I *do* feel like I've known you for a long time. It's made me rude," Torey said.

"Apology accepted. On that, I need to get moving. Full day ahead." Fawn popped the collar on her coat.

The sunny day had deceived them, and the wind's bitter breath gave her goose flesh. Torey's braids blew across her face before she tucked them under her scarf.

She put her hands in her pockets. She had such a delicate heart-shaped face and full, kissable lips. Her facial tattoo was of small petals traveling from her right temple to the apple of her cheek. Moreover, she didn't put on an act.

"It was great meeting up with you." Fawn released a sigh. "Thanks for the coffee."

Fawn interviewed people for honest currency, and she could tell.

Torey was genuine.

Briscoe sipped the first hot bit of his honey syth tea as he watched Fawn come in. She hung up her coat and satchel bag without so much as a good morning or grunt. Tomorrow she'd clean out her desk and deactivate her regulator chip. He swallowed and took another sip to dissolve the lump of emotion.

"You're here early," he said in way of greeting.

"I had to be up early." Fawn sat down and rolled up to her desk. She swept her fingers across the smart-glass to wake up her computer. "Before you ask, yes, it was to meet with Torey, and no, I don't want to talk about it."

Briscoe raised his eyebrows. "You look troubled. What's going on?"

"It's bugging me how Dr. Baldwin got the bot to murder Dr. Cho. We don't have any evidence." Fawn scanned pages as she swept through the electronic files on her smart-glass.

"If we can't prove it, it could mean there's nothing there. You're clutching at straws."

"I can't see the bot stalking and killing him on its own volition. It would take an awareness n-bots don't have."

"Yeah, but Cho had altered several of them." Briscoe shrugged and adjusted himself in his chair. The leather crinkled beneath his weight. "He gets it wrong, and it kills him. That's it."

Fawn shook her head. "He was a robotics expert…"

"And human." Briscoe drained his tea. "You had coffee?"

"Yeah. I'm good." Fawn sighed, but her jaw muscle throbbed. "I got a feeling about this, BB. Something's not right."

"Stop me if you're heard this before, but we don't confirm violations on feelings. You're obsessed and, like you said, we don't have any evidence."

"We're an obsessive bunch, regulators." Fawn rolled her eyes and spun around in her chair. "I'm not going to get this resolved before tomorrow."

"Death violations don't work on our timetables. Mario will find something."

"In the meantime…"

"You'll tell me about the breakfast date." Briscoe smiled.

"Ummm, no. How about we look for evidence?" Fawn tilted her head to the side. "You know. Our job?"

"How? The AGEH won't let us speak to Dr. Baldwin again. No judge will grant permission to search their facilities due to all the tentacles the meds have in everything." Briscoe stood up. "Imma gonna go get food."

"No Raul?"

"No, he worked late last night, and I didn't want to wake him." Briscoe waved as he left.

He let out a sigh at the memory. They'd had some tension since his attack.

Raul had tumbled in around two, raw and ragged. He'd showered first thing before he fell into bed.

Briscoe started down the stairs to the first-floor canteen. With Raul's frustrated cries echoing in his mind, Briscoe gripped the railing.

The greasy aroma hit Briscoe like a fist. Baked bread and eggs from the smell of it. His belly rumbled in agreement. Once seated, he ate the bowl of eggs and warm toast. Briscoe chewed and drank more tea. The weak, watery syth tea tasted like it had sat on the shelf for more than a few years.

The chair across from him screeched as Regulator Daniel Tom lowered himself into it. "IR Baker, can I join you?" Daniel placed his mug on the table next to his tray.

Briscoe nodded, since the inspector was already seated. He'd seen Daniel around but their interactions were slight. His tan skin held hints of copper and his light brown eyes twinkled as if amused.

"So how's your violation going?" Daniel popped a piece of what looked like fried tofu into his mouth. His plate contained a heap of tomatoes and cucumbers. The GMOs were getting better every year.

"Still under investigation. Yours?" Briscoe asked.

"Concluding." Daniel leaned forward. "How's IR Granger?"

Briscoe swallowed his swig of tea. "Why?"

"Oy! The serious look on your face." Daniel raised his

hands in a 'don't-shoot' position before lowering them. He grinned. "I'm just making conversation."

"Making conversation is asking me how I'm doing or how's the weather. You're digging. Tell me why you wanna know about her?"

Daniel laughed. "Damn, Neese said you were a bulldog when it comes to her. Look, I've heard some things and I wanted to see if she was doing okay after all the drama this week."

Heard some things? From Neese, no doubt.

Briscoe put his fork down and pushed his plate away. "You're saying a lot of words, but none of them answer my question."

"There's nothing sinister about it. Granger's cool people. I like her. Okay?" Daniel ate a few more tofu pieces but kept his gaze on Briscoe.

"She's good, and she's leaving." His words came out sharper than he intended. Briscoe adjusted his shirt.

Jealousy made people mean. Neese and other inspectors liked to taunt Fawn for that reason alone. They teased her about the incident, using it like blackmail to hold over her. So, yeah, he'd grown a bit protective of his partner.

Daniel continued eating but nodded his head in acknowledgment. Once he finished chewing, he said, "I know. She's a solid inspector. We're losing a good regulator. I couldn't get Damoni to talk, but she did."

"True. You got that right." Briscoe narrowed his gaze at the junior inspector. Daniel Tom didn't fit what he'd expected from Neese's partner. He had hidden depths.

Clattering caught their attention, making them jump.

When they spied the cause, a clumsy server with an armful of dirty dishes, they looked at each other and chuckled.

Daniel eased back into his seat and clucked his tongue. "The lawyers are working with Damoni to get her some deal."

"This is the informant —or hacker person—you and Fawn picked up?" Briscoe wiped his mouth with handkerchief.

"Yeah. Here's the thing. She has intel on the AGEH." Daniel pointed a crisp tofu square at Briscoe before tossing it in his mouth. "It could possibly help with your death violation."

"Why would she share any intel she had with us? She's got The District over a barrel."

Daniel smacked his lips as the ice cubes rattled in his glass. "What?"

"What I mean is, whatever information your hacker has on them, it'll never see daylight in a courtroom. If I was you, I'd petition to have her moved to witness protection, give her a new identity—record and backup all of her information before the AGEH makes her vanish. Permanently."

"You make them sound like they're above the law." Daniel laughed. Despite his laugh, he sounded annoyed and agitated. "You don't know Damoni Brees."

Briscoe cleared his throat. "And you don't know the AGEH. Tangling with them is not gonna end well."

Daniel got up. He collected his tray and, with a glance back at Briscoe said, "You're a gloomy bloke, but you dress brightly."

Briscoe beamed. "*Merci*!"

Two hours later, Fawn stood on the AV Media floor, at the Crypto department desk.

"Mario transferred a malfunctioning n-bot from a violation scene for a code review."

Regulator Kim nodded behind her VR goggles. "Right." She scanned the tele-monitor embedded in her desk. "He asked Regulator Ripley to finish the manual review and comb the code. They're in back on left, console 36. Let's do the security check before you head back."

"Thank you." Fawn allowed the facial scan and voice print match before Regulator Kim waved her on.

Briscoe completed the same security measures.

She headed down the rows, checking the electric number placards. *What did they find out?*

"Be ready for the results. The machines don't lie."

"Let's just see what they did find, okay, BB?" Fawn grimaced. She didn't want to snap at her partner. He just wanted her to avoid disappointment. Although she sounded confident, the knot in her stomach said different.

They reached console 36. "Regulator Ripley?"

"Yeah." Regulator Ahmad Ripley pushed their goggles into their dark hair. They didn't get up from their bucket seat, but they greeted Fawn and Briscoe with a nod, eyes locked on the screen. A bank of thin, clear monitors sat in rows of three—all held info.

"Granger and Baker? Right?" Ripley didn't wait for an answer. The n-bot's image appeared on screen before winking out and being replaced by lines of code. "Inspector Regulator Granger, you look like shit. You used to be so handsome."

Fawn followed their finger to the now highlighted code on screen.

Ripley was standoffish, like many in the crypto section, but they did crack a smile.

"I see you still have stale jokes," Briscoe said.

"Ouch." Ripley placed a hand over their heart.

Briscoe laughed before he caught an elbow to the ribs. "Oof! Fawn!"

"See here. You can find little pieces that can mislead you." Ripley got right down to business. They pointed at the screen.

A groan formed at the back of her throat. Fawn stood up straight.

"But see here," Ripley added. "This is the original coder's identification, a signature if you will."

All is not lost. Fawn looked over their shoulder again.

"Here. Employee code LC3671793." Ripley reviewed the line. "This is the bot's programmer. It looks like this person added additional command lines and a subroutine around security."

"The third arm," Fawn said.

Ripley nodded. "Yes."

"No sign of other programmers?"

"Yes, of course. These nurse bots are collaboratively

built. But the programming around the modified specs is this one employee's code." Ripley swept the screen and began sending it to her. "That's our assessment."

Seeing the conversation's end as Ripley disappeared back into their work, Fawn and Briscoe left.

Ripley's insight re-framed the case into a clearer picture.

It didn't mean she liked it.

Briscoe touched her shoulder. "Don't be distraught. The AGEH will get theirs."

"They're a vile organization, just like the Human Rights League." She crossed her arms to keep from punching something. She couldn't shake the feeling Dr. Baldwin had lied to them. but even if she could prove it the falsehood, it wouldn't be evidence to support a death violation conviction.

"We'll keep at them. Remember, battles win wars." Briscoe gave her a one-arm hug. "Come on. It's about lunch time and I know you didn't eat breakfast. Let's go get some good pho."

CHAPTER SIXTEEN

FRIDAY MORNING ARRIVED TOO SOON for Fawn. She stood in her office with a mug of black coffee. For now, a hushed quiet blanketed their shared space. The death violation had kept her from collecting her personal items and packing up her desk.

She'd come in early to do it but found herself staring at the death violation board. It was over. Dr. Cho's death had come at the mechanical hand of his own modified nurse bot.

With a heavy sigh, she removed items from the screen, dragging them into the Leonard Cho death violation folder. The jpegs, their notes, the interviews—recorded and audio—and CCTV clips. She swept them all into the yellow electronic folder on the screen's virtual desktop. It saved to the cloud and backed up to a remote site.

"You're early," Briscoe said as he came into the office.

He carried a cup of steaming liquid in one hand, and a cigarette in the other. His messenger bag hung on to his right shoulder for dear life. "I thought I was the early bird."

"Morning to you. I wanted to get a jump on all my stuff." She gestured at the container in her chair.

"Right." Briscoe sat his cup down, extinguished his cigarette in his desk's foghog, and removed his bag. As he took off his coat, he avoided eye contact with Fawn.

"BB…" Fawn started but couldn't find the right words. Nothing would make her leaving any easier.

When Briscoe turned around from hanging up his coat, he huffed. "I had all these plans for an office party and a goodbye spray across your desk. You know, good luck and all that, but then I realized last night, I didn't mean it. I don't want you to go. I don't want you to have good luck at your new job. I want you to miss me and regret it."

Fawn's eyebrows shot into her hair. "Thanks for your honesty."

Briscoe flopped down into his chair. "I know. It's selfish, but it's how I feel. Of course, I don't want you to hate your new job. I already know you'll be great at it. I just…"

"I know," Fawn said. "Change is hard."

"And sometimes unnecessary." Briscoe picked up his cup and sipped.

"Excuse me. Am I interrupting?" Dr. Rycroft stood just inside their office doors.

He held his tablet to his chest. He looked from Fawn

to Briscoe and back again. His auburn afro stood at peak roundness, and his black sweater revealed a rather lean and muscular torso and biceps. He wore black slacks as well. Seeing him in casual clothes, minus the lab coat, made Fawn smile.

"No, come in." Briscoe waved him inside.

Dr. Rycroft did as suggested and walked over to the chasm between Fawn's and Briscoe's desks. Fawn could see that his intelligent eyes held their usual sharpness despite the early morning.

"Inspector Regulators Granger and Baker, I wanted to get the final report on Dr. Cho's death violation from vioTech to you. I know it's your last day with us, IR Granger."

Fawn pursed her lips and moved the container from her chair. Somehow, she wanted to be seated when Dr. Rycroft gave his final report. He looked worried, and his hands clutched the tablet in a death grip. She probably wasn't going to like what he had to say.

"Well?" Briscoe said.

"Dr. Cho's death violation is closed. The manner of death, laser-gun blast to the chest caused massivetraumatic cardiac arrest. My final findings are Dr. Cho's cause of death was accidental. The victim altered the nurse bot's programming and it killed him." Dr. Rycroft glanced up at Fawn.

"A man does not program a bot to kill him and then fight it off!" Fawn smacked her hand on the desk. "Despite what Regulator Ripley found in the code."

"It doesn't. The nurse bot malfunctioned," Dr. Rycroft explained in his quiet tone.

Fawn scoffed. Saying it softer didn't change his report. "Accidental."

"Yes." Dr. Rycroft held his tablet back up to his chest as if protecting himself. "There's no evidence to the contrary. I wish I had better news for you."

"Fawn." Briscoe came over to her. "Cho modified the code. It only proves he did it. You heard Rycroft. We don't have any evidence proving it *isn't*."

Dr. Rycroft nodded in agreement. "Dr. Cho modified a nurse bot, turning it from a medical device into a security machine. That machine malfunctioned. He tried to defend himself, and it killed him. The damage to the machine caused it to crash near him. The evidence dead ends—excuse the pun—there."

"I know you hate to admit it, but Rycroft is right." Briscoe crossed his arms. "When bots malfunction and people are killed, they're always labeled accidental. There's a precedent set for it already."

Fawn eased into her office chair. "Think about the damage medical nurse bots that are actually armed weapons could cause. The carnage. You can't tell me that a large corp like AGEH wouldn't move on that tech? The District's defense ministry would love that. No humans needed for war."

Once Briscoe returned to his desk, he lit a cigarette. "It's all conjecture, Fawn."

The bots were completely devoid of human compassion.

"Dr. Cho was the victim of someone's rage," Fawn said.

"Nothing we have supports your theory," Briscoe

said. "Most death violations fall into one of three categories: greed, lust, jealousy. Cho's death doesn't hit any of those, which means it isn't an intentional death, but an accidental one."

"You know the AGEH has something to do with this." Fawn looked at Briscoe.

"You're letting your feelings block your clarity."

"Me? Are you sure it isn't you?" Fawn tapped her neck, signaling to Briscoe's hatchling tattoo.

Briscoe stiffened. As a hatchling, his existence derived from the AGEH's program. "*Touché*. Still, we follow the evidence. We did that and this is where it led."

Briscoe always cut to the quick. Fawn lowered her head.

"I'm sorry, BB." She shouldn't have used his hatchling status against him. It was immature and mean.

Dr. Rycroft looked uncomfortable. He glanced around the room before bringing his eyes back to her. "Well, this is goodbye, Inspector Regulator Granger. Best of luck on your relocation. It's been great working with you."

"I'm not relocating." Fawn realized she meant it.

He paused; a smile tugged at the edge of his lips. "You're not?"

"No." Fawn sighed.

After her talk with Torey, she had done more soul-searching. She could treat her PTSD with The District's physicians the same as she could elsewhere. Here she had a support system, and she knew the community. The job caused her stress, but she wouldn't run from her illness. More than that, The District was home. It was in her bones.

"You're staying?" Dr. Rycroft's smile emerged in full. "Good. I 'd like the opportunity to work with you again. We need sharp minds here."

"Seems like you're going to get your chance." She smiled in return. His grin had become infectious.

"Until then." With a look back at her, Dr. Rycroft exited their office.

Briscoe cleared his throat. "What was that all about? You're not resigning?"

"No. I'm not." Fawn leaned back in her chair.

Briscoe s tapped on his desk. "What's going on? You've been looking forward to that ranch for years."

"I'll tell the Southwest Regs to keep the position. At first, I was sparks out about The District, but this case...well it rekindled my fire. This is my territory. I won't abandon it."

"You sure about this?" Briscoe peered across his desk at her.

"I am." Fawn reclined in her seat.

"You're serious?"

"Yeah. Gotta go tell the captain."

"Huh, look at that." Briscoe looked at his smart-glass monitor.

"What?"

"Damoni Brees has escaped the holding cells and is now missing. The TRU unit is attempting to locate her." Briscoe took a drag of his cigarette.

Fawn shook her head. "Interesting. Neese and Daniel will be tied up for a bit."

"Good. 'Cause there's a death violation over in sector 14 for us…" Briscoe got up and went to pull on his coat.

"Fine, but it's your turn to write up the Dr. Cho report." Fawn put on her own coat.

Briscoe blew a stream of smoke. "Deal."

The End

READY FOR THE NEXT DEATH VIOLATION?

READ ON!

BONUS EXCERPT FROM IMMORTAL PROTOCOL: DEATH VIOLATIONS 02

Betrayal begins with trust.

The clicking keys sounded like tap dancers echoing inside Fawn Granger's apartment. The entire sector had been carved out of abandoned warehouse buildings and converted into little boxy living spaces. Tucked inside her bedroom, Fawn, sweaty, with dry lips and eyes burning in fatigue, sat hunched over her wireless keyboard. Darkness blanketed everything beyond the edge of the blue LCD illumination pouring from her laptop.

"Slow down." Briscoe, her partner in The District Regulators, said into her ear. The earpiece distorted his usual whining, but Fawn still heard the uptick of annoyance.

"Can't." Her fingers tapped out the command string for the deep web search.

"You gotta rest. We been chasing this for hours," Briscoe muttered. "Not counting all the days last week."

"So. Close." Fawn's fingers were a blur across the keyboard. Her dreadlocks fell into her eyes. With a quick head toss, she moved them back out of her way.

She didn't have time to stop, to think about what to say to Briscoe. Words took time, which was in short supply at the moment. Beneath her shoulder holster, her white tee-shirt clung to her, and her body reeked from sweat, but showering, eating— and yes, sleeping —had to wait.

Citizens lives depended on it.

Her discomfort—and Briscoe's for that matter—be damned. Overhead, a lazy ceiling fan spun, completely ineffective against the raging muggy heat. The sweltering summer seeped through the thin walls and weak insulation. Stuffy and sticky, Fawn blew out a huff. The building's air conditioner had given up.

"If we can catch The Fish, we can stop the killings." Fawn typed faster, fingers aching, tendons screaming from overuse. "Don't let me down, BB Just a few more minutes. Then the trace will pinpoint his location."

Briscoe Baker, or as Fawn liked to call him, B.B., sighed. "We've been here before. So damn often we should start paying rent. We get to the location and it's a dead end. We've taken The Fish's bait, and he's dragging us through the internet's choppy waters. *Again.*"

Fawn watched the flashing green dot on her screen. As it pulsated, it sped through the map of The District, like a heat-seeking missile. It latched on to The Fish's wireless signal and chased it. Briscoe meant well, and they *had* done this so many times Fawn had lost count, but this time would be different.

She knew it.

"No more deaths," Fawn whispered, mostly to herself and to the dark lining the edges of her room. The laptop's light only went as far as her knees before succumbing to the shadows. Not too long ago she had almost walked away from the work of regulating The District's sectors. She'd been sparks out of patience and her Post-Traumatic Stress Disorder had left her fragile and wounded, despite the A.I.'s mandated mental health sessions and her medications.

The last several months she had focused on herself and her trauma. It was exhausting but necessary work.

She still owned the ranch in the Southwest Territories. It waited. Calling to her. Sometimes, on her more difficult days, she almost answered that call. But something about The District's citizens and its ugly underbelly demanded cleansing. It kept her here, tethered to the murkiness.

"Death is what we do, darling," Briscoe said, with a small thread of amusement in his tone. Always the comedian.

Fawn shook her head. "No. Death is why we send people to sleep in The Cradle."

Briscoe didn't respond. Instead, the clicking of keys emitted from the earpiece. She heard him breathing, but something had snagged his attention away. She prayed it was something worthwhile for once. Not that he liked talking about The Cradle—warehouses lined with banks of people in tubes, filled with flotation, stasis-inducing gel. An A.I. attempted to rehabilitate them through mental therapy.

Fawn shuddered and pulled her attention back on the subject at hand.

Lurking in her assigned sector, someone enjoyed hurting people.

The Fish.

A faint stir in the sticky air made Fawn pause. With her fingers hovering above the keyboard, she cocked her head sideways and listened.

There. Barely audible came what sounded like the rustle of paper.

Fawn uncoiled from the bed, slipping one foot to the wood floor and then the other. She knew her apartment like the back of her hand, and she crept across the area rug, her footfalls quiet and certain in the shadows.

Whoever had infiltrated her space didn't. The advantage would be hers.

She picked up her laser-gun from the nightstand where she'd placed it, and waited beside the automatic door.

"Fawn? You there?" Briscoe asked, concern made his voice hard. "Fawn!"

"Quiet!" she hissed back.

The bedroom door slid open.

Fawn held her breath and readied her weapon.

In padded her black cat, Sebastian. She let out a breath.

"You scared me half to death!" Fawn scolded, scooping Sebastian into her arms and cuddling him. With the weapon in one hand and the cat in the other, Fawn laughed. "You'd better not have made me miss The Fish."

"The cat? You scared *me*!" Briscoe grumbled. "You can change the settings for the door to not go crazy when the cat's about."

"But I heard something else." Fawn searched the living room from the doorway. It too lay in gloom, with only the coffeepot's illumination burning a bright green in a sea of black. Nothing moved. Fawn frowned. "I could've sworn I heard something non-cat related."

"You want me to come over?" Briscoe asked. "I can be there in six."

"No, no I think I'm good." She wished she sounded as sure as her words.

With that she replaced her weapon on the bedside table and returned to her bed. Checking that the gun was within arm's reach, Fawn picked up the keyboard with one hand, and sat down again. Once she released Sebastian, she got back to work.

"Okay. Where are you?" she whispered.

The pulsating dot had been swallowed up in the sea of scarlet lines, black blocks, and blue elevated lanes that crisscrossed the screen in an attempt at an electronic Jackson Pollock painting.

"It stopped in the Adams Morgan area, Sector 12." Briscoe sounded about as excited as paint drying on cargo craft.

"The 12. The Fish is down in The 12. Grab those coordinates and meet me there." Fawn yanked on her pants and slipped her feet into her Regulator-issued boots. They had steel in the toe, and they protected her feet when she had to kick something or someone.

"Sector 12 isn't in our scope, Fawn."

"Just meet me down there."

"See you in fifteen." Briscoe ended the connection.

"Make that ten." Fawn put her arms through a fresh tee-shirt.

She left her apartment, taking the stairs down six floors to the basement and her aerocycle, a sleek dual wind-powered machine. It used electricity to power its wind turbines. She threw her leg over, jammed on her helmet, and took off toward the elevated lanes.

Now she'd snare The Fish.

Want more? Get your copy of IMMORTAL PROTOCOL today!

YOU MAY ALSO ENJOY

The first Kingdom of Aves Mystery

The Cybil Lewis Science Fiction Mystery Series

The Soul Cages: A Minister Knight of Souls Novel

NICOLE GIVENS KURTZ'S TITLES

Death Violation Cyberpunk Series

Glitches & Stitches

The Butterfly Nexus

Kingdom of Aves Mysteries

Kill Three Birds

A Theft Most Fowl

Cybil Lewis SF Mystery Series

Silenced: A Cybil Lewis SF Mystery

Cozened: A Cybil Lewis SF Mystery

Replicated: A Cybil Lewis SF Mystery

Collected: A Cybil Lewis SF Collection

Minster Knights of Souls Space Opera Series

The Soul Cages: A Minister Knight of Souls Novel

Devourer: A Minister Knight of Souls Novel

Candidate Science Fiction Series

Zephyr Unfolding: A Candidate Novel

Weird Western Anthology

Sisters of the Wild Sage: A Weird Western Collection

As Editor

SLAY: Stories of the Vampire Noire Anthology

Made in the USA
Columbia, SC
05 October 2023